# INTO THE LION'S DEN

"Get out of here—and close the door behind you," Lord St. Claire ordered Kate, when at last she managed to find him in a remote room in his London mansion.

Kate did close the door—but from the inside. She did not want servants to overhear what she had to say to St. Claire. She then proceeded to tell him in no uncertain terms that it was his duty to return to the ball that his mother had arranged, though Kate could guess how unpleasant he might find it.

"You are good at guessing—as when you found me here," he said. "Innocent Kate, in your pretty green gown."

Then, without warning, he pulled her forward, one arm enclosing her in a band of steel, the other lifting her face to his, his mouth closin███████████first, robbing her o███████████til her lips parte███████████a trembling ecs███████████e.

Kate might ha███████████;— but she never would have guessed she could feel like this. . .

# Kate and the Marquess

—∿—

*by*

Sheila Walsh

A SIGNET BOOK

SIGNET
Published by the Penguin Group
Penguin Books USA Inc., 375 Hudson Street,
New York, New York 10014, U.S.A.
Penguin Books Ltd, 27 Wrights Lane,
London W8 5TZ, England
Penguin Books Australia Ltd, Ringwood,
Victoria, Australia
Penguin Books Canada Ltd, 10 Alcorn Avenue,
Toronto, Ontario, Canada M4V 3B2
Penguin Books (N.Z.) Ltd, 182–190 Wairau Road,
Auckland 10, New Zealand

Penguin Books Ltd, Registered Offices:
Harmondsworth, Middlesex, England

First published by Signet, an imprint of Dutton Signet,
a division of Penguin Books USA Inc.

First Printing, August 1997
10  9  8  7  6  5  4  3  2  1

# One

Children's laughter, drifting on the March breeze, reached the upper windows of Kimberley's West Front. The sound, so joyously uninhibited, brought an instant smile to the Dowager Marchioness of St. Clair, who occupied a suite of rooms in the West Wing when she was in residence. Her drawing room, with its Chinese rugs and chintz-covered chairs and hangings, was generally acknowledged to be one of Kimberley's most charming and comfortable rooms, though her recent incapacity due to a twisted knee presently rendered it more in the nature of a prison.

However, the laughter from the gardens below lifted her ladyship's spirits. Impulsively, she reached for her stick, but hardly had she grasped it, let alone attempted to rise, when a thin, wispy woman who had been sitting in a corner beside the hearth flung aside her tatting and sprang to her feet.

"My dear ma'am, pray do not, I beg of you . . ." she cried, clutching at her shawl which threatened to slip to the floor. "Only tell me what it is you require . . . and I will fetch it in a trice. Doctor Andrews was most insistent that you should rest . . . such a shock it must have been . . ."

"Doctor Andrews is an old woman," declared the marchioness, grasping her stick firmly as she came to her feet. "And as for being shocked, I hope I am not so poor-spirited. Goodness me, I have nothing more than a slightly sprained knee, due entirely to my own carelessness in failing to look where I was going. It is already much less painful, and a little exercise can only be beneficial . . ."

"If you say so, your ladyship," Miss Priddy twittered, hovering uncertainly. "Though I'm sure I shall not know how to face his lordship if any further damage should be sustained."

Lady St. Clair wore her years lightly, with no trace of gray in her pale gold hair, and looking, so her son, Blaise, avowed, too ridiculously young to be a dowager. She was also blessed with a generous disposition, and knew full well that her impatience with Miss Priddy, who was, after all, only performing her duties, if a trifle overconscientiously, was born of frustration.

Poor Priddy. She had been so different before that terrible mishap last year, when she had inadvertently become locked in the disused family chapel all night. An overzealous keeper, finding the door open and the chapel apparently empty, had suspected one of the gardener's boys of larking about, and had locked the door.

It had never become quite clear why she had gone there in the first place. From her hysterical and somewhat incoherent ramblings, in which bats figured quite prominently, it appeared to have had something to do with a history of the house which she had found in the library, penned by a cleric over a hundred years earlier, concerning an ancient triptych said to be concealed behind the altar. Having been something of a bluestocking in her younger days, this had excited her interest, and upon finding the said triptych, she had not heard the keeper call, being wholly engrossed in deciphering the inscriptions.

Although physically unscarred by this experience, the Miss Priddy who had originally come to Kimberley as a stimulating companion for Lady St. Clair, following the death of her dear husband, was now a nervous shadow of her former self, her fine mind reduced to a hesitant jumble. Her ladyship, assuming responsibility for what had happened, felt compelled to keep her on indefinitely, there being no family to take responsibility for her. And Blaise, though less sympathetic, raised no objection.

"My son comes home so seldom these days that I doubt he will learn of my indiscretions," she said more kindly now, her sigh of disappointment swiftly veiled. "But should he do so, dear Priddy, I promise that no blame will attach to you. So, be a dear, and oblige me by humoring my odd quirks," she concluded coaxingly. "I wish only to go as far as the window so that I may watch the children. Perhaps you would oblige me by setting a chair there for me."

As Miss Priddy hastened to oblige, the marchioness limped across to the window. Kimberley was set upon high ground and it was generally agreed that the West Front had the finest views of all, with the gardens below falling away in a series of terraces which in summer were a riot of color. At ground level they were bounded by a wide, semicircular driveway, leading to an ornamental lake on the one side, the glint of water just visible through a grove of lime trees, and on the other to the main entrance, while a lesser path carried on to the Home Wood and the stables.

The marchioness drew aside the curtain and saw her two grandchildren running around and around the terraces in pursuit of an enthusiastic puppy of dubious ancestry: Lord Freddie, at almost six years of age, very much in charge, with the little Lady

Roseanne, whose delicate constitution had caused them so many sleepless nights, trotting behind, determined not to be outdone—a tiny doll-like three-year-old, the very image of the mother she had never known.

Their state of happy abandon would have brought instant censure from their governess, Miss Glynn, but in her absence it drew no such disapprobation from the slim young woman who watched them, her laughter mingling with theirs. She wore an olive green pelisse which looked well on her, while a matching bonnet, already discarded, swung carelessly from one hand, thus freeing a cloud of flame-colored hair which had escaped its pins and was being whipped about her head by the strong breeze.

"That will do now, children." Her voice carried faintly on the breeze. "You'll have the poor wee doggy overexcited."

Her voice came faintly to their grandmother, and she smiled involuntarily, for Kate was the image of her mother at nineteen.

Lady Elizabeth Welby had been her dearest friend—still was, though they had not met for some years. They had shared their come-out—how long ago it seemed. Elizabeth had been the acknowledged beauty that Season, though her sunny nature had robbed her of any conceit. She could have had the pick of any one of the eligible bachelors who laid their hearts and their not inconsiderable fortunes at her feet. Elizabeth had smiled kindly on them all before confounding everyone by eloping with an impoverished young Irish doctor, Patrick Sheridan, who was in London to further his studies.

It had caused a dreadful scandal at the time, the marchioness remembered, but Elizabeth had never regretted her decision, and now lived in happy

simplicity a few miles outside Dublin, where
Patrick was now an eminent surgeon, surrounded
by a brood of children, of whom Kathleen Alicia,
her ladyship's godchild, was their eldest daughter.

*When last we met, dear Alicia,* Elizabeth had written at Christmas, *how long ago it seems, you very
kindly begged me to send Kate to you to make her come-
out if I could not manage it, but that was some years
ago. We even harbored plans for her and poor Blaise, as I
remember . . . so sad, the way things have turned out.
Please God, he will come to terms with his loss eventually. But if you now feel that having Kate would be inappropriate, do not hesitate to say so. I shall quite
understand, and try to make other arrangements . . . my
parents would have been the obvious choice, but Papa,
having set his face against me, has cut all ties, so that I
have finally given up writing to Mama. Kate, of course,
thinks the whole idea is a shocking waste of time and
money, but there are few if any eligible young men in
Balwinny, and Patrick and I are both determined that
she should at least have her chance . . .*

And so she shall, vowed the marchioness, watching the girl below gather the children and the
puppy, and set off in the direction of the Home
Wood. She sighed. If only Blaise could be brought
to see that life can sometimes offer one a second
chance, if only one is prepared to meet it halfway.

Two castellated lodges guarded the main entrance to the house, together with a pair of ironwork gates whose stone pillars were fashioned in
the likeness of twin lions rampant, their front paws
upholding a magnificent ironwork arch, proclaiming to the world in gold letters two feet high that
this was Kimberley, for two hundred years the
country seat of the St. Clair family.

The country lane following the boundary wall
meandered peacefully beneath white scudding

clouds. Thick hedges, which in autumn would be laden with hawberries, separated the lane from the farmland beyond, while within the gates stretched the Long Mile, lined with military precision by the famous Kimberley elms, now fat with buds, planted by the third marquess and said to be more than a hundred years old. And in the far distance, on rising ground beyond a belt of woodland, stood the house itself, serene, majestic, its windows glinting in the sunlight.

The serenity of the afternoon, however, was presently shattered as the distant summons of a horn brought two servants scurrying from one of the lodges to throw wide the gates. Their task was barely accomplished when, with a rush of loose gravel and hoof, a gleaming black curricle with bright yellow wheels drawn by four high-couraged, perfectly matched black thoroughbreds rounded the sharp bend in the narrow lane, driven by an imposing figure wearing a many-caped drab greatcoat that proclaimed him to be a much-envied member of the Four Horse Club. Without slackening pace he swung his excellent equipage through the open gates, judging the distance to an inch.

"God help us all!" muttered Jem Briggs, picking himself out of the holly bush where he had landed. "No thought for others. Kill hisself one day, 'e will, and us along of 'im."

"There's them as reckons that's what he's been tryin' ter do ever since that sweet lady, 'is wife, was took," muttered his companion. "But by the powers, 'e can drive to an inch!"

Pogson, who had caught the tale end of this rodomontade, glanced at the young man beside him as they sped down the Long Mile. The well-bred countenance beneath the fashionable high-crowned beaver betrayed no sign of his having heard, but had he done so, he would have affected not to care. Pogson had been groom to his lordship since the day he rode his first pony—such a merry boy he had been then—more than twenty-six years ago, it was—and in that time he had seen the best and the worst of Blaise, sixth Marquess of St. Clair.

There had been times, right enough, in those early days following on the death of his sweet lady wife, when his lordship had been sufficiently wild with grief to contemplate ending it all. But, God be thanked, not by putting others at peril. It just wasn't his way.

Even so—he glanced aside at his lordship's profile with its now pronounced air of careless arrogance—the tragedy had left its mark, right enough. But women of a certain kind seemed to find his new care-for-nothing manner irresistible. He could have his pick of such women, and frequently did—very expensive little lovebirds they often were, too. But it was a bird of a very different plumage as had ruffled his lordship's feathers this time—one of his own kind (always a mistake, in Pogson's view) who, having been free enough with her favors, had suddenly turned virtuous and demanded respectability. And the marquess, furious at having the tables turned, so to speak, had departed Town in high dudgeon.

Above them, the branches whipped about wildly in the March wind, but the marquess showed no immediate disposition to slacken speed. His initial fury had cooled somewhat, though its cause still rankled: that he, who had always conducted his affairs with discretion, concluding them generously and without rancor, had come perilously close to allowing himself to be outmaneuvered by a conniving woman.

The marquess swung the curricle hard left at the end of the Long Mile. "We'll cut through Home Wood to the stables," he said, easing off on the

reins with the glimmer of a smile as he saw that his
groom was clinging to his seat. "Pace too hot for
you, is it, Pogson?"

"I hope I may not be thought so poor-spirited,
m'lord," Pogson returned with the injured air of
one whose courage has been cast into doubt. "But,
what I says is, there's a time and place for such displays, m'lord, and the Home Wood ain't one of
them."

Irritation flickered and died in the marquess's
face, to be replaced by one of his swift, rare grins.
"Still ready with the timely rebuke, you old stickler? Ah, well, point taken." He eased gently back
on the reins as the rough path curved around to
meet the sweep of the drive leading to the stables.

The wheels and the beat of the horses' shoes on
the rough ground muffled all sound, so that he was
afforded no warning as a small excitable ragamuffin of a dog came scampering toward him, trailing
its lead. Upon seeing four snorting monsters bearing down, the animal skidded, its mouth open in a
soundless yelp of terror, and shot off into the
bushes.

"Hell and damnation!" exclaimed the irate marquess, instinctively hauling back on the ribbons.
But his anger turned to blind panic as hard on the
wretched animal's heels came two small all-too-
familiar figures, followed almost immediately by
an older girl, her flame-red hair flying in the wind.

In the ensuing pandemonium, the girl, with a
presence of mind that he was too angry to appreciate, pushed the children willy-nilly into the bushes
in the wake of the dog, and followed after them
with more speed than grace. At the same time, Pogson, helpless to intervene, hung onto his seat as the
wheelers endeavored to kick in the panels beneath
his feet, while the marquess, with every ounce of
skill he possessed, fought desperately to keep con-

trol. Mercifully, having traveled fast and far that day, they responded more quickly than might have been feared, and with one final superhuman effort he managed to drag the team to the off and bring them safely to a standstill. Pogson immediately leapt down and ran to the wheelers' heads, soothing them with soft words until, recognizing his voice, they lost much of their panic.

His lordship, however, experienced no such relief. He was white-faced, shaking with rage and the suppressed recognition of his own culpability— and not a little with the still lingering horror of what might have been. The sounds of tears and youthful voices raised in protestation of their innocence, mingled with the constant yapping of the dog, served only to fuel his wrath.

His six-year-old son was the first to emerge, his clothing disheveled, his face scratched and streaked with dirt, and his cap askew as he struggled manfully to contain the squirming body of the shaggy dog, which was no more than a pup, his face betraying a confused mixture of eagerness and apprehension as he became aware of his father's thunderous expression.

"Pa! It's you! We didn't . . . are the horses all right?" At this point, his enthusiasm overcame all else. "I say, that was the finest piece of driving ever!"

"Don't try to toad-eat me, Frederick. It will be no thanks to you and that reprehensible animal if the team is not lamed. Furthermore, you may think yourself lucky that I didn't run you down, which is no more than you deserve."

The boy flushed painfully. Pa only called him Frederick when he was really angry. "Oh, but you wouldn't have . . . Pogson once told me that you had the safest pair of hands of anyone—and he should know!" With great daring he concluded,

"Besides, you aren't being fair! How were we to know . . . it all happened so fast . . ."

"That will do!" thundered his father. "I want no excuses."

"But Freddie isn't making excuses. It wasn't his fault that the puppy slipped his lead."

Unnoticed, the older girl had also emerged, bringing half the undergrowth with her by the look of it, a bonnet much the worse for wear swinging carelessly from her wrist. She was carrying a whimpering, white-faced Roseanne, talking softly to her. The marquess saw that she was older than he had at first thought—more woman than girl, in fact. The face now lifted to him with the cloud of red-gold hair drifting across it, had a freshness, a liveliness about it, which owed much to her eyes, which were as clear and green as a deep mossy pool, fringed with long dark, gold-tipped lashes. They were also, he noted, brilliant with indignation.

"Do you say so, miss?"

"I do. Sure, it wasn't poor Freddie's fault that Cormac slipped his lead. It's a trick puppies learn very young, as I'm sure you'll allow, and there didn't seem any great harm in it, being on private land and all. In fact, to be honest, I'd say that you were equally to blame, for, to be sure, that was no way to be driving a team of horses in a place where anyone might be taking a walk. And such fine horses, they are, too. If they were mine, I would have more of a care for them."

There was a palpable silence. Pogson could not recall anyone who had been so foolhardy as to question his lordship's skill with the ribbons. He stole a glance at his master—saw that his heavy brows had descended until they almost met his narrowed, glittering eyes. The groom held his breath and waited for the storm to break.

"Would you, indeed?"

The silky-soft words penetrated Roseanne's sobs, which increased in volume. Kate shivered involuntarily. She had spoken in haste, and out of a desire to defend Freddie. But now she had a terrible premonition that her impetuosity was about to be her undoing. Oh, glory! If looks could kill, she thought, I'd be dead and buried, for sure. An apology would be wasted on the man in his present mood. Besides, she had gone too far now to draw back.

"I would so," she returned defiantly, above the hiccuping sobs of her charge. "Roseanne, *achushla*, hush now, you are not hurt at all. It was just a big adventure, and if you cry, you will frighten poor Cormac, for he is still only a baby, and not a big girl like yourself." She set the child down, brushing her down before removing the worst of the twigs and dead leaves from her own person. Then, almost certain that a fine old row was brewing, she said firmly, "Freddie, take your sister and the little dog back to the house. And, for pity's sake, keep tight hold of the lead this time. I will be along directly."

"One moment." The marquess's voice was like chipped ice. "Where, pray, is Miss Glynn?"

"She had to go home, Pa, to nurse her mother, who is ill," Freddie said quickly. "But Kate is looking after us splendidly."

"Is she, indeed?" His sarcasm was biting, fueled by his daughter's frightening pallor. "That is a highly debatable assumption, my boy. But I shall have more to say about it later. Go now. Look after Roseanne, and make sure that mongrel is well confined until we decide what's to be done with him. Not you, miss," he said to Kate. "I have not nearly finished with you."

Kate flushed angrily and Freddie looked mulish and set to take issue, but she forestalled him, urging him to do as his father bid him and hurry home before Roseanne took cold.

When the children had gone there was complete silence once more except for the restless movement of the horses. Kate was mortified to find herself in such an ignominious position. Why could she not have realized sooner that the man she had accused of reckless driving was Freddie's father? The boy's initial exchange with his parent had rather passed over her in her preoccupation with Roseanne, though she ought to have guessed. But the marchioness had made no mention of the marquess's coming, and it had simply never occurred to her. Such things she had said to him! Not that she was sorry, for indeed they were nothing less than the truth. If only he would speak and get it over.

To break the silence, she walked over to where the groom was still calming the horses. "Are they quite recovered?"

"Ah, just about, ma'am." Pogson, unlike his furious master, instinctively recognized quality and touched his hat. "They're high-couraged cattle, y'see, an' it give them a bit of a fright."

"Yes, it would. Oh, but they are beautiful."

Kate moved closer to the leaders, ignoring his muttered warnings as she did the marquess's sharp order to her to "Come away, girl. Haven't you done enough damage for one morning?"

The thoroughbreds showed the whites of their eyes as she approached. Pogson held his breath, afraid to act for fear of making matters worse. She was talking to them softly in a strange lilting tongue, so close now that she was almost nose to nose with Prancer on the near-side, their breath mingling. And they became as gentle as kittens.

"Well, dang me if I've ever seen the like!" he muttered, as she moved on to Prince. "I've heard tell of such things . . . but . . . dang me!"

"Our old groom back home reckons it is the music of the language," Kate said softly. "Don't ask me how it works, for I don't know myself. But they'll be just fine, now, the beautiful creatures that they are."

She stepped back, for the moment could no longer be put off, and turned to glance up at the marquess. He was tight-lipped and white around the gills, and Kate shivered involuntarily. *May the saints preserve me, for he looks mad enough to kill.* But to do so he would have to climb down from the curricle, and that would unsettle the horses again. So she was able to address him with more bravado than true courage, looking him straight in the eyes.

"I believe you had something you wished to say to me, my lord. Shall we get it over with, before the horses take a chill from standing so long?"

*If marquesses could erupt like volcanoes,* she thought belatedly, *this one would be spitting fire any minute, for sure.* But as she waited for the torrent to descend, he treated her to a long savage glare, ordered Pogson to climb aboard, and drove off, leaving her barely enough time to leap out of the way. *Well really,* Kate thought, *such a display of temper!*

She was not sure whether to be relieved or apprehensive as he disappeared in a cloud of dust. But of one thing she was certain—that would not be the end of the matter. There would be a reckoning later, as sure as God made little green apples.

Even so, and in spite of their differences, Kate was reluctantly obliged to admire the quality of his driving, and his restraint in not allowing a raging temper to affect his handling of the ribbons.

# Two

Kate took the back stairs to her room, lest she should encounter the marquess. Naturally, she could not hope to avoid him for long, but long enough perhaps to allow the worst of his anger to abate.

With the cool light of reason fast asserting itself, she was obliged to admit that she had not behaved well. No, that was an understatement. She had behaved abominably. That he had been almost equally at fault afforded her little comfort.

No doubt at this very moment his lordship would be voicing his grievances to his mother. And, Kate acknowledged miserably, who could blame her if she took his part, fair-minded though she undoubtedly was. To be sent back home in disgrace would be too awful, not because she would mind missing the Season—she had never cared about that in the first place—but the feeling of having let everyone down, her parents, the marchioness, and, not least, herself. She sighed.

The only course open to her was an apology. It would stick in her throat, and he would probably refuse to accept it, but she must attempt one with as good a grace as she could manage and hope for the best.

There was a soft knock at the door, and Annie, the nursery maid, put her head in. "The children were asking if you were back, Miss Kate. They're just finishing their tea and I think they was wanting you to come and tell them one of your stories."

Annie's own wanting was in the plea. She was little more than a child herself with her thin wiry body, and her big eyes, dark and round with expectation. Miss Kate was a great teller of stories—Irish fables, she called them—but to Annie they were pure magic.

"Will their father not wish to see them?"

"Oh, he's been up already. Been and gone in a matter o' minutes." Annie lowered her voice. "In one of his black moods, he was, too. Myrtle, who brought up the tea, had it from Art, one of the stable lads, as his lordship'd had a bit of a set-to with some intruder in the Home Wood. Mad as fire, he was, seemingly, when he reached the stables— though no one rightly knew what had happened as Pogson wasn't givin' much away."

Kate made some vague comment and hoped her discomforture didn't show. She glanced at the little clock on the mantelshelf. Four o'clock and the marchioness usually dined at five.

"Well, perhaps just a very short story. Tell them I'll be with them in five minutes."

It was close on five when Kate made her way downstairs. She had taken more than usual care with her appearance in an effort to boost her confidence. Her hair was coiled up into a sleek knot on top of her head, and secured with a prettily ornamented Spanish comb that her mother had given her before she left home.

"I had it for my own come-out, dear," Mama had said mistily. "I remember I wore it the night I first met your father. Perhaps it will bring you your heart's desire, too."

There was little likelihood of that, Kate thought

ruefully, but it gave her a little mock courage. Her high-necked dress of pale green crepe was simply cut, making her appear, though she herself was unaware of it, at once taller and more fragile. A pin set with seed pearls placed at the neck of her dress was her only adornment, apart from a scarf of beautifully worked Irish lace which she wore draped across her arms.

The drawing room door was slightly ajar. She paused to draw courage and the marquess's voice came clearly to her.

". . . I could scarce believe my eyes to find my children running wild like ragamuffins, lessons abandoned, ill-disciplined and left to the attentions of one of your lame ducks. This one was Irish by the sound of her, and as brash, self-opinionated and impertinent a hoyden as ever I saw . . ." Kate stood, rooted with indignation. ". . . Furthermore, I must make it plain that I do not care to have them left in the charge of one so totally devoid of manners . . ."

"And I do not care to be lectured by you, my dear, much as I love you." Lady St. Clair's tone was remarkably restrained, though cool. "As for Kate . . . I assume you are speaking of Kate"—this was said with particular emphasis—"Elizabeth's eldest girl, and my goddaughter, though one would scarcely recognize her from your description, for she is a delightful girl and totally unspoiled—"

"You would not say so if you—"

"Pray, do not go on, Blaise," her ladyship commanded. "You may say something you will bitterly regret. It surely cannot have escaped your memory that I am to bring Kate out during the coming Season. Which will be a great joy to me, I may tell you, for she has been here less than a week, and already, simply having her about the place has brightened my days immeasurably."

"Mother—"

"As for the children," she swept on imperiously, "their lessons have not been neglected. In fact, Kate reckons that Freddie is a bright child who has reached the point where his mind needs stretching. She wondered whether, if you are agreeable, Mr. Pargeter, the curate from Brinkley, might be willing to come in three mornings a week to tutor Freddie—scarcely the suggestion of a harum-scarum hoyden. However, that is not a matter of great urgency. What is more important, to my great joy, Freddie and Roseanne are learning how to play, and it is my opinion that they are happier and healthier now than I have ever seen them under Miss Glynn's rather repressive regime—excellent governess though she may be—and this transformation is due entirely to dear Kate, who understands as I do that although children need discipline, they also need to run a little wild occasionally."

Kate thought that this might be a prudent moment to make her presence known. But before she could move, the marquess was off again.

"To which end," he ground out, "this paragon of yours has also allowed them to acquire, from God knows where, a misbegotten, out-of-control shagrag of an animal which is undoubtedly flea-ridden, and riddled with every conceivable disease—"

Kate could bear no more. She pushed open the door. "I'll have you know, my lord, that it was I brought Cormac as a gift. I chose him specially from my own spaniel's litter, and far from being misbegotten, his sire happens to be a particularly fine Irish wolfhound. Furthermore, if you weren't so ill-tempered and hasty in your judgments, you might have discovered what a little darling he is, and full of character, which is why I named him after one of the great warrior kings of Irish legend . . ."

She stopped as abruptly as she had begun, though her cheeks burned and her eyes still sparkled with the force of her grievance as they challenged his. So much for an apology, chided the small voice of reason. But she was not sorry.

In the silence that followed, a faint gasp came from Miss Priddy who, enveloped in folds of gray muslin, had shrunk quivering into her chair, at once dismayed and awed by Kate's lack of deference toward his lordship. A furtive glance at his face revealed eyes, more black than blue, fairly blazing with anger beneath lowering brows. This brought a fresh spasm to her thin body, so violent that it was like to play havoc with her digestion. In her agitation, her headband with its nodding plume slipped askew, and she was obliged to straighten it before fumbling in her reticule for her smelling bottle.

At which point the butler announced dinner.

"Good," said the marchioness with, Kate could swear, a twinkle in her eyes as she reached for her stick. "Blaise, perhaps you would be so kind as to lend me the support of your arm as far as the dining room."

"By all means, Mama. Then, if you will excuse me . . . ? From one cause or another"—he cast a fulminating glance at Kate—"I find I have little appetite."

"That would be a pity, my dear." The marchioness's spoke pleasantly, but there was no mistaking the faint undercurrent of censure. "I am well aware that you are used to keeping Town hours, but although I daresay Cook will understand why you feel unable to partake of her excellent cuisine when the matter is explained to her, it must nevertheless appear as a slight, don't you think? You have always been her particular favorite, as you are very well aware . . ."

It was the most decided set-down. He flushed and threw her a look of exasperation. "Enough, Mama. You have made your point."

As they processed to the dining room, Kate found herself torn between admiration for the marchioness and pity for her son, though the rebuff was richly deserved. She decided that it was the prominence of his nose, together with those extraordinary eyebrows, that gave him such a haughty air, making his arrogant profile more than usually pronounced as he acknowledged his mother's discreetly veiled reproof.

All in all, it was an uncomfortable meal, though Lady St. Clair kept up a flow of conversation to which Kate responded when required to do so with as much aplomb as she could muster, aware that his lordship, while toying broodingly with his pheasant, and refilling his wine glass rather too often, was observing her every move, analyzing every opinion expressed by her. It put her on her mettle, determined that he should have no cause to find fault with her a second time.

It had been Kate's intention to escape as soon as dinner was at an end so that the marchioness might have her son to herself. However, having escorted his mother as far as the drawing room and seen her settled, the marquess forestalled her by making his excuses, and this time her ladyship reluctantly accepted them. In a sudden impulsive gesture, he stooped and kissed her cheek with a degree of affection that made Kate wonder whether he might perhaps have some redeeming features. While she was still wondering, he bowed stiffly to Miss Priddy and herself and left the room.

"If you would not mind, dear ma'am," exclaimed Miss Priddy, gathering up her tatting and her

shawl, and all her other bits and bobs, "I rather
think that I, too, should like to retire to my
room . . ." She stood up, dropping her tatting in her
haste. Kate moved swiftly to pick it up for her. "So
kind, my dear," she said, gathering it in with the
rest. "A trifling headache—oh, nothing to cause
alarm, I assure you, dear Lady Kimberley—and I
know that Miss Sheridan will look after you admirably in my stead . . ."

"Poor Priddy," said the marchioness, as the door
closed behind her. "She tries so hard and has been
so good to me since I twisted my wretched knee."
She leaned forward, lowering her voice. "In fact, I
dare swear that if you had not arrived when you
did to lighten my days, her kindness would by
now have worn me to a thread!"

Kate laughed, and came to sit on a low chair
nearby. She said ruefully, "Your son does not view
my presence kindly, I think. Though I was a wee bit
outspoken when we met earlier this afternoon, so
we got off to a bad start. I hadn't the first idea who
he was, d'you see, until I'd said my piece, and after
that, it was too late and matters just went from bad
to worse. And I swear I had every intention of
apologizing, but . . ."

"Pray, do not even think of apologizing, my dear.
I know my son well enough to believe that he deserved every word." The marchioness sighed, and
a note of pleading entered her voice. "You must not
mind Blaise, my dear. He was not used to be so in-
tolerant. It might surprise you to know that less
than five years ago he was as charming, good-
natured, and out-going a young man as you might
wish to meet."

Kate thought again of their first stormy encounter and his subsequent behavior, and wondered if they were talking about the same person.

She decided that allowances must be made for a mother's partiality.

"That would be before his wife died?"

"Yes." The marchioness sighed. "Poor Lucinda. She was a delightful creature—the light of his life. But even then she was delicate. Freddie was born when she was not quite twenty. It was a difficult birth and although Freddie was a sturdy baby, Doctor Andrews advised against attempting any further pregnancies. I believe that Blaise has never forgiven himself for letting Lucinda persuade him to go against that advice, for Roseanne was born two months early, such a tiny scrap we none of us thought she would live."

"But it was Lucinda who died," Kate said quietly.

"I believe it was quite the most dreadful moment of my life, worse even than my own dear husband's death the previous year." Lady St. Clair pressed a lace handkerchief to her mouth.

Kate leaned forward impulsively, exclaiming. "Dear ma'am, pray don't! Don't speak of it, if it upsets you so."

"You're a good child. But you need not fear that I shall become a watering pot. It will do me good to speak of it. Edward was some years older than me, you see, and he had enjoyed a good life. I still miss him, of course, but I have always consoled myself with the notion that Edward died on the hunting field, doing what he loved best. But Lucinda . . ." She sighed again, deeply. "That was different. She had all her life before her . . ."

"Have you perhaps considered that, had she lived, she might have been a permanent invalid?"

"Dear child!" The marchioness stretched out a hand to her. "Doctor Andrews said the very same thing. But Blaise could not accept any hint of mitigation. After Lucinda's death, his whole personality seemed to change. In retrospect, I believe he came close to losing his reason, and for that I cannot but feel some degree of blame. I was so preoccupied with Roseanne at the time, you see—we all were; such a frail, wee doll of child, she was, clinging to life by a thread—that I believe I neglected to notice his odd behavior—his reluctance to even look at his daughter."

"It is a not uncommon reaction in such circumstances, dear ma'am," Kate said softly. "My father has met it many times."

"I am sure you are right, my dear, for Blaise did come 'round in the end, except . . ." She hesitated, as if unwilling to portray her son in a bad light. "He became very protective of her, obsessively so, but from a distance—do you understand? It is almost as if he is afraid to love her as he loves Freddie."

Kate leaned forward, staring into the fire, seeing again that arrogant face as she had seen it earlier in the day, suffused with anger. But, before that, in those first moments when the horses were close to stampeding, had she not also glimpsed a moment of blind terror? The marchioness's outpourings in no way excused his behavior, of course, but they did perhaps afford some explanation of his violent reaction.

The older woman studied the pure line of Kate's profile etched against the flames, and it was as if the years fell away, for she was so very like Elizabeth in many ways—impetuous, lively—her ladyship smiled—and with the same fiery temper when roused. The marchioness had met Elizabeth's doctor-husband only a few times, but he had impressed her with his quiet, steadfast air of determination, and she sensed that Kate had inherited some of that same resolution.

"I am sorry that your first meeting with my son

was so unpropitious, my dear," she said, rousing
herself to appear more cheerful. "But if you can
manage it, try not to judge him too harshly. For
myself, I can only take heart from what you have
told me of his behavior, for he spends so much time
in town now, that I had almost begun to believe
that he had schooled himself to care for nothing."

"He cares for you," Kate said swiftly. "One can
see that at a glance."

"Oh, yes, I believe he does," sighed the marchioness. "But I shall not always be here." Her
voice lightened suddenly. "However, I refuse to re-
linquish the hope that in time his heart will find
room for someone else. In fact . . ." She hesitated,
looked intently at Kate, then said brightly, "No
matter, my dear. And now I believe I should like to
retire—if you would be so good as to pull the bell
for Bertha."

When her ladyship had departed with her maid,
Kate found herself unable to settle. It was too early
for bed, and in any case her mind was far too busy
with all that her godmother had told her to contemplate sleep. In the end, she fetched her serviceable frieze cloak from her room, changed her
pumps for a stout pair of shoes, and let herself out
by one of the side doors.

It was a cold, clear night with a touch of frost,
moonless but brilliant with stars. She wrapped the
cloak around her and strode out quickly to keep
warm, through the grove of limes and across the
wide expanse of grassland, already crunching
slightly underfoot. The sounds and the smells were
endearingly familiar, so redolent of all that she
most loved, that as she approached the lake which
gleamed blackly, mirroring the stars above, a sudden wave of homesickness threatened to overwhelm her.

What am I doing here, she thought, when I could

be back in Balwinney with everyone I love, and them loving me? Kate shut her eyes and pictured the family: her mother and father sitting quietly together in the comfortably shabby drawing room, and the twelve-year-old twins, Michael and Calum, fast asleep in their cozy room under the rafters, while her sisters, practical fourteen-year-old Mary, and Deirdre, who at sixteen was undoubtedly the beauty of the family, would be in the room below, whispering their secrets to one another in the safe anonymity of darkness. And close by, darling Meaveen, the baby of the family, who had brought great joy to everyone four years ago, arriving when her mother had long since given up any thought of adding to the family. Would they be missing her, too? Enough to maybe give her a thought now and then?

And what of Kit, her eldest and dearest of brothers, whose exploits in the war against Napoleon Bonaparte had been commended by Lord Wellington? He had returned home briefly a week or so before she left for England, newly promoted and as devil-may-care as ever, and full of stories about battles that made his young brothers' eyes sparkle, and set them playing at sword fights with sticks until her mother had forbidden them. "They'll have one another's eyes out, if they're not killed first!" she had protested, and when Kit laughed, she had drummed her fists against his chest until he caught her to him. "And you should be ashamed of yourself, encouraging them!" They had all ended up laughing, but the tears were not far away. And all too soon, with an extra hug and a kiss for herself, Kit was away to rejoin his regiment.

Tears hovered on her lashes and she drew her cloak more tightly about her, for only yesterday there had been a rumor in Brinkly that Bonaparte had escaped from Elba and was on his way to reclaim his lost kingdom . . . returning, as he had vowed, with the violets. If it were true, Kit would no doubt greet the news and the prospect of renewed fighting with an enthusiastic hurrah . . .

"Who is there?"

The peremptory challenge shattered the silence. The voice was unmistakeable. Oh, glory! Of all the people she least wished to meet at this moment! But there was no escaping him. As she was slow to answer, his shadow loomed. He took her arm in a vicelike grasp, and swung her around, pushing back her hood.

"You again!" he exclaimed. "What the devil do you think you are doing out here alone at this hour?"

Kate swallowed the lump in her throat, striving for lightness. "Much the same as you, I imagine, my lord," she said huskily. "Taking the air. Though I'm bound to confess that if this is how you are minded to treat your guests, I shall be more circumspect in future."

She glanced meaningfully down at his hand, which still held her in an iron grip. He released her so abruptly that she almost fell.

"You are my mother's guest, Miss Sheridan, not mine. No guest of mine would be so foolish as to stray so far from the house at this late hour." He loomed over her, so close that she could hardly fail to be aware of the faint aura of brandy fumes. "Good God, woman, do you not realize that my gamekeepers patrol these grounds at night to deter poachers? You seem determined to put yourself in peril. First my horses—now this!"

Was it anger or the brandy that made his voice shake? Unaccountably the lump was back in Kate's throat, and her own voice was a little thick and not quite steady as she answered him.

"I am not as stupid as you seem determined to think me, my lord. As it happens, I am in no danger. I have an understanding with your head keeper, who is well aware of my liking for a late night stroll. Back home, you see, I am used to going out at any hour without fear of being set upon." She could not see the effect of her words, but the atmosphere was palpable. "However, I assure you that in future, I will be doubly careful. Good night, my lord."

"Not so fast." As she turned to go, his hand shot out again to detain her. Ignoring her protest, he pushed back her hood. "You have been crying."

"No, my lord."

"Yes, Miss Sheridan." The marquess removed his glove and drew a finger across her cheek. "Assuredly, you have been crying. Strange—I had not thought you the crying sort."

"Nor am I, sir," she returned, stung by the faint note of mockery in his voice. "But we all have our low moments, and this just happened to be one of mine."

He was silent a moment, then said in an odd voice, "Because of me?"

"No!" she exclaimed. And repeated firmly, "No, indeed. It is nothing, truly. A trifling attack of homesickness—nothing more. Please let me go, my lord."

He was slow to release her. But finally he stood back with a mocking bow and allowed her to pass.

# Three

The stables were already alive with activity when the marquess strode in just as dawn was breaking. There were lads polishing tack and cleaning out the long row of stalls set at right angles to the main building, and grooms could be heard whistling as they went about their work, swearing crudely and colorfully as they dodged the flailing hooves of the more restless horses.

No one but Pogson was allowed near his lord-ship's matched carriage horses, for they were high-couraged animals, given to being more temperamental than most. The groom was just giving Prince's coat a final buffing when he heard that familiar impatient stride echoing on the flagstones, and his lordship's voice upraised. The other horses heard him, too. There was a general shuffling and whinnying and Prince began to caracole.

"Easy, now, young fella-me-lad," Pogson admonished quietly as he nimbly side-stepped a flailing hoof. "He'll be along to see you soon enough, like he alus does before he takes his morning ride. An' I only hope as he's in a good mood, for it'll be heaven help us all if he en't." Reluctantly, he put down his brush. "No sense puttin' off the moment, I suppose."

Pogson's arrival initially went unnoticed, all sound being drowned out by Cormac's ecstatic

yelping. "Well, dang me!" he said softly, totally un-
prepared for the sight of the marquess standing in
the stable yard in the act of lifting up the children's
pup until they were eye to eye, at which point he
admonished the excitably squirming bundle to "Be
quiet, you reprehensible ill-disciplined little shagrag! Have you no discrimination at all?"

For answer, the puppy tried to lick his face. "No,
I see you haven't," the marquess said in disgust
and handed the unrepentant miscreant to the red-
faced stable lad. "Enough. Take him away, Jeb, and
tie him up firmly this time. He'll need to learn the
meaning of discipline if he is to remain."

"And is he to remain, m'lord?" asked Pogson,
coming forward.

The marquis swung around, caught in the act,
and not quite able to hide his embarrassment. And
just for an instant the groom caught a glimpse of
the happy, caring boy he had once been. The look
was gone in an instant, but it gave one to hope.

"That depends," came his lordship's austere
reply. "He needs a firm hand, and God knows if
he'll get it with everyone making such a ridiculous
fuss of him."

"No, m'lord," said Pogson, straight-faced. "Quite
so."

The marquess gave him a sharp look, but said
only, "I'll take Silver out this morning, Pogson. Get
him saddled up, will you? It's deuced cold standing about here."

There was an odd silence, broken only by the
yelping pup.

"Well? Go to it, man. I have no wish to freeze to
death."

"No, m'lord."

"And, for pity's sake, don't keep 'no, m'lord-ing'
me."

"No, m'—" Pogson cleared his throat. "The thing is, we have a bit of a problem."

"What kind of a problem?"

"Seemingly . . . while we've been away, and not knowing when we was due back . . ." With mingled relief and despair Pogson turned to the head groom, who had just come in from inspecting the stalls. "Ah, Harry, just in time. His lordship was wishin' to ride Silver."

"Damnation!"

The muttered expletive did not escape the marquess, any more than did the look that accompanied it.

"If there is a problem with my gray gelding, Masters," he said silkily, "you had far better come clean."

"Well, it's not a problem as such, m'lord," stuttered the discomforted head groom. "Leastways, not in the way your lordship might be fearing. In fact, the gelding is in excellent health . . . never better, what with all the reg'lar exercise he's been getting." He stole a glance at the marquess's face and looked away again swiftly. "It's just . . . well, the thing is, m'lord, Miss Sheridan took a powerful fancy to Silver, and the feelin' being mutual, as you might say—"

"Are you trying to tell me that Miss Sheridan has been in the habit of riding my prize gelding, man?"

"Every morning, m'lord, early as you please," the wretched head groom admitted. And as if to placate his master's anger, "He'll not come to any harm, m'lord, sure as I'm standin' here. Miss Sheridan's as bonny a rider—fer a female, that is—as I've seen in many a day."

"Miss Sheridan may be as competent as the devil himself, but even you must be aware that Silver can in no way be classed as a suitable mount for a lady."

"In general I'd have to agree, m'lord. But Miss Sheridan manages 'im a treat."

"Does she, indeed?" The silky voice was there again. "And, do I take it that Miss Sheridan is out on Silver now?"

"Yes, m'lord. Left some fifteen minutes since."

"And which direction did she take?"

Masters hesitated. "She was heading toward Brinkly, m'lord."

"Then, be so good as to saddle Ebony Boy—and be quick about it."

Within minutes, the marquess was on his way, fairly flying across the fields until he disappeared into the copse.

"Why did you have to tell him which way she'd gone?" asked Pogson, feeling unexpectedly sorry for the young woman.

"Because I want to keep my job, that's why," Harry Masters returned shortly. "We don't all enjoy a privileged relationship with his lordship, same as you do."

Kate had spent a restless night fraught with dreams of black horses galloping toward her at breakneck speed—of running helplessly after a small child only to see her tossed into the air like a rag doll. She woke early, soaked in perspiration.

The terror soon faded, but with it went all desire for sleep. Finally she rose and padded across to the window to drag back the heavy curtains. It was a gray, chilly-looking morning, but the frost seemed no heavier than it had been the night before, so she decided to dress and take her morning ride a little earlier than usual.

Her dark tan riding habit had seen better days, but it was made of good enduring Donegal tweed that would keep out the coldest winds. And her neat little black hat had a long scarf attached to the

back that one could wrap around against the cold
Irish mornings.

"You'll be needing a new habit for your London
debut," her mother had insisted when Kate had returned from a ride shortly before leaving home.
"Something really stylish. But it can go on the list
with the rest. Alicia always had excellent taste."

"That list is growing as long as Casey's tongue,"
Kate had protested, only half laughing. "Sure,
you'll have poor Pa ruined, the way you're aiming
to spend his money on me. And for what?"

And she had turned to the mirror, where she saw
a slim young woman whose features, though regular enough to please, had too strong a bone struc-
ture to merit true beauty. Furthermore, just now
those same features were unfashionably glowing
with health due to a recent and most invigorating
gallop. "I mean, just look at me. Gentlemen aren't
interested in healthy young women. They much
prefer some pale ethereal creature like Eileen Monahan, who simply asks to be cherished, and to
whom they can pen romantic verses," she had said,
adding without a trace of envy, "And I couldn't
look ethereal in a million years, even if I wanted to,
could I, now?"

Kate did not add, as she might have done, that a
wee fortune might just constitute sufficient induce-
ment to tempt a greedy man, but that to be married
for money would, to her, be worse than remaining
a spinster. Nor could she voice the wish closest to
her heart—that, were it not impossible, she would
dearly like to follow in her father's footsteps and
become a doctor.

Even so, her mother had found her reasoning absurd. "The Eileen Monahan's of this world are like
sweetmeats," she had said dismissively. "Delicious
on the tongue and gone to nothing in a moment.
Very unsatisfying. Whereas you, my dear, are a

lovely, warm, and caring girl, with the kind of beauty that endures because it comes from within—as any gentleman worth his salt will soon discover for himself."

Kate was ruefully aware that the partiality of a mother's love must blind her to an objective view, for it was a partiality that few gentlemen would endorse, if pressed to be honest. Ah, well, she thought, they must take me as I am, or not at all, for I won't dissemble in order to please.

She reined Silver back as they approached a ford in a stream that was deeper than usual due to a recent heavy rainfall.

"Good boy," she murmured, patting his neck as, after a nervous little jig, he began to pick his way across, sure-footed. "You're a fine brave fellow, right enough." But he had barely gone halfway when the sound of hoofbeats coming at full gallop unnerved him and set him caracolling, churning up the water.

"Damn the fool, whoever he is," Kate muttered, suppressing her fury as all of her energy and skill were channeled into controlling a now thoroughly agitated Silver.

Finally, she coaxed him up and out onto dry land where, with a mixture of firmness and sweet reason, she managed to rein him in. Only then did she allow her own feelings to surface. She wheeled around to give her pursuer the length of her tongue, and found herself looking into those deep-set blue eyes that mirrored her own fury.

"What the devil did you think you were trying to do with my horse?" he thundered.

Silver threatened to become overexcited again upon hearing his beloved master's voice. "Easy boy," Kate murmured, patting his neck until he calmed down again, by which time the marquess had dismounted and tied Ebony Boy to a tree. She turned to face him as he strode toward her, striving to contain her own anger for fear of setting the horse off again.

"I wasn't *trying* to do anything, my lord. I was, in fact, quietly and patiently encouraging Silver to negotiate the swollen ford—with reasonable success, I venture to say, until you came charging up like the cavalry in full flight, frightening him half to death. If I had been less experienced, and he less intelligent, he could well have had me in the water with himself—and maybe kicked me half to death."

"Which would have been no more than you deserved," the marquess ground out, glaring up at her with a hand firmly on Silver's bridle.

"Oh, how unjust! And ungracious!"

The fact that she was right on all counts did nothing for his lordship's temper. He was only too aware that from the start he had allowed irrational anger to override all other considerations. Also, he had been riding much too fast as he approached the stream, which had probably unsettled Silver, but instead of pulling up and trusting animal and rider to extricate themselves safely, he had precipitated a situation which might, without Miss Sheridan's undoubted skill, have ended in tragedy.

He looked up to see her stroking the horse's neck and murmuring those strange soothing words to him, much as she had done to his carriage horses yesterday.

"Silver is not a lady's mount." His voice was tight, almost surly.

"Maybe not. Or just maybe it depends on the lady, for we get on just fine together."

The horse, hearing the marquess speak his name, whinneyed and began to nudge at his coat.

"Will you look at that, now." Kate leaned forward suddenly, the hint of a smile in her eyes as her anger evaporated. "Isn't he the bright one? I daresay you are in the habit of keeping an apple or somesuch in that pocket for him . . ."

And as the marquess half-guiltily pulled out the said apple which Silver delicately lipped off his hand, she laughed—a whole-hearted joyous sound that drew a reluctant smile from him, prompting her to say impulsively, "Ah, listen, now, I know we got off on the wrong foot entirely yesterday—and I'll admit that I was as much to blame as you . . ." One of those fierce eyebrows shot up, and she grinned ruefully. "Well, a wee bit more so, maybe. I'm a great one for speaking before I think, and many's the time it's got me into trouble." She reached out her hand. "But could we not make a fresh start—for your mother's sake, if for no other reason. She sees you so infrequently, and because she loves you, it distresses her when you are unhappy."

For a moment Kate thought she had said too much, for he hesitated, frowning. Then he leaned across and found his own hand firmly taken in a friendly, no-nonsense clasp. It came as a surprise, though on reflection, it was clear that a limp maidenly handshake would not be her style at all. He looked up to find her watching him with frank interest, and realizing that he still held her hand, he dropped it like a hot coal, and turned away to untie his horse and swung himself into the saddle.

"We had better ride on before the horses take a chill."

"Yes, indeed," she said, though she made no move to do so. "But before we do . . ."

He frowned. "Well?"

"It's only . . . well, the thing is, I have no intention of luring Silver away from you—not that I could if I tried," she amended hastily. "But I would still like to ride him occasionally, when you aren't here—if you have no objection."

"Whyever should I object, Miss Sheridan? The horse needs regular exercise, and you seem to know what you are about."

Kate ignored the heavy sarcasm. "That is probably because I could ride almost before I could walk. I find it by far the most convenient way to get about in Balwinney." She glanced across at him. "So, you are quite happy for me to ride Silver?"

The marquess seemed to sigh. "Happy? Ah, now that is a different question altogether. But yes, Miss Sheridan, you have my permission." He glanced from her to the gray. "The two of you would seem to enjoy a natural rapport."

"We do, don't we?"

She swung Silver alongside him and they set off at a gentle canter. For a while neither spoke. The sun was coming up, bathing the frosted landscape in its golden light. Away in the distance, the spire of Brinkly church pierced the morning air, and it, too, was tinged with gold.

"Doesn't such a morning make you glad to be alive?" Kate said, drawing the deep cold air into her lungs. When he didn't answer, she glanced across at him. His face was tightly drawn, expressionless, and she cursed her clumsy tongue. "It never quite goes away, does it?" she said quietly.

He shot her a frowning, questioning look.

"I had a sister. Almost exactly a year younger than me, she was, and the two of us close as twins." Kate seemed to be talking to herself as much as to him. "When she was fourteen she contracted scarlet fever, and not all of Pa's knowledge and love and undoubted skill could save her." Her voice thickened slightly. "I took the fever too, but less severely. And although it is quite illogical, I have never quite been able to forgive myself for recovering when she did not."

She looked across at him then, her lovely green

eyes brilliant, her throat tight with unshed tears. Even so, she managed a tremulous smile. "Sometimes, even now, she feels very close, and I still get angry, but I do try not to let bitterness erode the happy memories."

The marquess was shaken to the core, not knowing if his own anger was directed at her for preaching at him, or against the cruel fate that had robbed him of his dear love.

"My mother talks too much." He ground the words out in tight-lipped fury.

"Oh, never say that! Your mother cares! She told me what happened, yes, but only, I think, to explain why you—" Kate stopped as impulsively as she had begun, one glance at his stony profile making her aware, too late, that she was treading on perilous ground.

"Oh, pray do not boggle at plain speaking! You have gone much too far to draw back now." Ebony Boy also sensed his lordship's pent-up emotions. His ears went back, and he began to pull on the rein, and Silver, picking up the vibrations from his voice, jinked nervously.

"I'm sorry, my lord," Kate said, subduing her own feelings in an attempt to calm things down. "Perhaps I should not have spoken as I did. Pray, believe me, it was not meant as a criticism. Our cases are very different, after all . . . there can be no possible comparison . . ."

"No." His voice was low, anguished. "No possible comparison."

An awkward silence ensued, which Kate, learning from her previous mistake, made no attempt to breach. They had come around almost full circle, and were now approaching Kimberley, riding past the West Front on their way back to the stables.

"When do you go up to Town with my mother?" The question was abruptly delivered, but his voice had lost that anguished quality, and Kate realized with some surprise that he was trying to make amends for his lack of manners. Her own generous nature rose to the occasion.

"We hope to leave early in April, but only if Miss Glynn has returned—and if her ladyship is fully recovered, of course. She seems to think, as my own mother does, that I require a great many new clothes."

The amusement in her voice surprised and intrigued him. "And what does Miss Sheridan think?"

"The idea is very agreeable, of course, and it would be very odd in me to quibble. Though I cannot help but think it a great waste of Pa's money."

"An unusual philosophy for a young lady approaching her first Season."

"Perhaps. But then, the whole idea is a little absurd, don't you think?" A low trickle of laughter escaped her as she turned to meet his quizzical gaze. "My looks are unremarkable, and I have no fortune to recommend me—and even if I had, the very notion of parading myself in the hope of attracting a husband is anathema to me."

"Then I fear you will find yourself very much out of place among your contemporaries. For the majority of them, and their mothers, the hope of making a suitable match will be their sole *raison d'être*."

"If that is the case, then I am sorry for them."

"You are very severe, Miss Sheridan. And not a little contrary. Pray, why go through the motions if you are so set on spinsterhood?" he challenged her, his curiosity aroused.

"I didn't say I was averse to marriage, my lord," Kate returned with spirit. "Only to the Marriage Mart, as my mother calls it—to the whole concept, in fact, of becoming an object to be approved or found wanting. From all I have heard, fortune is the prize, and love too often plays a very small part."

For a moment she hesitated, wondering if the turn the conversation had taken might remind him of his own tragic marriage, which was undoubtedly a love match. But a quick glance reassured her, for the glint of amused disbelief in his eyes had not diminished.

"You are very severe in your assessment of us, Miss Sheridan. If you feel that strongly, why are you here?"

She had the grace to color, though she concluded with spirit, "I daresay it must seem odd that I should say one thing and do another, but both my mother and yours had set their hearts on my come-out."

"You could have refused."

"And spoil their pleasure?" She laughed suddenly as one of his extraordinary eyebrows described a wildly quizzical arc. "Oh, very well, I will allow that the idea amused and intrigued me. I have never been to England, you see—in fact, I've never been beyond Dublin in all my eighteen years and seven months. And, much as I protested when the idea was first proposed, I quickly realized that it was an excellent opportunity to visit London. I also thought it might be rather entertaining to observe how the fashionable disport themselves."

The marquess tried to visualize her among the fashionables, and came to the conclusion that she would either be a *succes fou* or a complete disaster. Only time would tell. As the stables came into view, he turned to her, his voice dry.

"I shall await your conclusions with interest, Miss Sheridan. As for our talent to amuse, I only hope you may not find us a sad disappointment."

She laughed. "I'm sure you could never be that, my lord."

# *Four*

April was well into its third week by the time Lady St. Clair was pronounced fully fit and ready to set off to London, by which time the rumors about Napoleon's escape from Elba had long been confirmed in two letters—one from Kate's mother and the other from a friend of the marchioness living in London.

"Eloise writes that he is already back in Paris, being feted by the people," her ladyship had said, perusing the letter yet again on the evening of its arrival, "and the King has fled across the border with his entourage—to a house in Ghent, so Eloise believes. She had it from Fanny Burney, whose husband, Captain d'Arblay, is with Bonaparte."

"How fickle the French people are!" Kate exclaimed, and found herself being eyed quizzically by the marquess. "Well, so they are!" she declared, unabashed. "Sure, it isn't a year since they couldn't wait to be rid of Napoleon, and welcomed King Louis with open arms."

"True enough," he agreed suavely. "But I fear *Louis le Desire* very swiftly became *Louis le Gros*, beside whom their returning Emperor must have seemed a veritable tiger."

"Will it mean war again?" Kate asked him, thinking immediately of Kit.

"Oh, undoubtedly, I should think." He saw the

momentary apprehension in her eyes. "Does the idea appall you so much?"

"It appalls all of us, I should hope," said his mother with unaccustomed brusqueness. "All those fine young men going back into battle—and Kate's brother among them."

"I'm sorry. I didn't know."

"Why should you?" Kate had managed a smile which didn't quite reach her eyes. "And, to be sure, I ought to be used to Kit's ways by now," she said overbrightly. "A soldier was all he ever wanted to be, and so far he seems to have led a charmed life, for he has come through all his previous campaigns without a scratch, so hopefully he will continue to do so."

The marquess, watching her, frowned, but made no comment.

The governess returned to take up her duties once more, her mother having recovered sufficiently to be left. The children greeted Miss Glynn's return with mixed emotions. They were not displeased to see her, but as Freddie had confided to Kate, "She's not half so much fun as you!"

"I hope you will not tell her so," Kate had said, trying to keep a straight face. "Her feelings would be dreadfully hurt, and I daresay I should get the blame for spoiling you."

"Oh, I won't breathe a word," Freddie promised earnestly, hand on heart, and looking in that moment of intensity the very image of his father. "Miss Glynn is not that bad, I suppose, and anyway, I shall be starting my lessons with Mr. Pargeter next week. Pa arranged it with him before he left."

The marchioness had hoped that her son might remain longer at Kimberley—might even be persuaded to escort them to London. But although he stayed rather longer than she had expected, he eventually began to grow restive, and was gone before a second week was out.

Kate wasn't sure whether to be glad or sorry. Roseanne still showed a marked tendency to cling to Kate's skirts when her father was present, which seemed to try his patience, though in mitigation, his lordship had begun to take Freddie around the estate with him more frequently, which pleased the marchioness. The young boy had returned from one such outing suffuced with pleasure, the words tumbling over each other.

"Papa is a great gun!" he enthused. "He says I'm to have my own pony as soon as a suitable one can be found, and Kenny, one of the young grooms, is to teach me to ride! And Papa ac-sherly picked Cormac up today and let him lick his face, so he must like him, really, mustn't he?"

Kate agreed that it certainly seemed so, though privately she would have thought more of the marquess had he put off his return to London until the new pony was found—perhaps even long enough to teach his son to ride, as her father had taught her.

"Blaise certainly spent more time with Freddie than he has ever done before, which must give one hope." Her ladyship watched Kate playing with the children. "If only . . ." She sighed. "But then, perhaps I am in danger of expecting too much, too soon."

The journey to London with the marchioness proved to be vastly entertaining. Kate's only experience of long-distance travel hitherto had been the uncomfortable crossing from Ireland in the company of one of her father's more distinguished colleagues, who had also accompanied her on the long drive, by mail coach, as far as High Wycombe, and thence to Kimberley by post-chaise.

Her ladyship's notions of travel, however, were vastly superior, and if they occasionally teetered on the brink of absurdity, Kate would not have dreamed of saying so. She was much entertained to discover that it required not one sumptuous carriage, but two, to transport three ladies and Bertha, her ladyship's maid, to London—the incoherent Miss Priddy having been invited to accompany them. "For although she is sometimes a little tiresome, I could not possibly deprive her of such a treat, my dear," the marchioness had confided. In addition, there was a positive mountain of baggage to be accommodated, enough to occupy the whole of the second carriage, among which Kate's own portmanteau squatted insignificantly, as if ashamed to be seen in such august company.

"But, my dear," the marchioness explained when Kate's astonishment became apparent, "we shall be away for the better part of three months, and one needs a great many gowns if one is not to appear tawdry . . ." there was a decided twinkle in her ladyship's eyes, ". . . to say nothing of bonnets and wraps and shoes. And then there are all kinds of pills and potions . . ." she continued, warming to her theme as Miss Priddy nodded earnestly, and Bertha uttered a decided sniff. "At my age, you know, one must be prepared for all eventualities . . ."

"Oh, pray, ma'am, do not go on!" Kate said, her eyes brimming with laughter. "To be sure, I am more than five, and know perfectly well when I am being bammed! Pills and potions, indeed! As if I haven't seen poor Bertha, here, struggling to persuade you to allow her to pack even a modicum of the medicine prescribed by Doctor Andrews."

"Pah! Colored water dosed with laudanum. A fine thing it would be had I allowed myself to be persuaded to take such a soporific on a regular basis. I should very soon have dwindled into a dozy old crone, and we would not now be on our way to London. Whereas, a moderate draught at night has enabled me to sleep, which is all I ever asked of it."

"And which same I have taken the liberty of packin', your ladyship, beggin' your pardon, being wishful not to be caught without it on the journey," declared Bertha, with a hint of truculence in her manner. "There'd be no Doctor Andrews to call on in some strange hostelry halfway to Lun'on if you was to be taken bad."

"Dear Bertha, you are always so thoughtful for my good. But I have no intention of being 'taken bad,' and there is nothing strange about the Red Lion at Plumford, as you well know. Edward and I stayed there often in happier times. And Blaise has made the reservations for us, and will have ensured that everything is as it should be. He offered to come home to escort us, but I told him I was not yet in my dotage."

"So kind of his lordship," Miss Priddy exclaimed, wishing that he might not so easily have been dissuaded, and nervously striving to banish visions of footpads and highwaymen, with no protector to vanquish them. She finally conquered her nerves and contented herself with diffidently expressed hopes that the sheets at the inn would be well aired. "For it would not do at all if your ladyship were to catch a chill."

"Of course the sheets will be aired, and I have no intention of succumbing to any kind of indisposition," declared the marchioness, stifling a strong urge to snap. At which point her eyes met Kate's, and the humor therein expressed enabled her to see the funny side.

The children had been allowed to wave them off. Roseanne had clung to Kate's skirts, her lower lip trembling, tears glistening in her lovely, long-lashed eyes in spite of all Kate's promises to return soon, and to write them a regular account of her doings. "And you will write back, Freddie, with your news. That way, the time will soon pass."

Freddie promised with great fervor, and scoffed at his sister for being a crybaby. But his own lip had quivered very slightly as Miss Glynn gently but firmly removed Roseanne so that his grandmother and Kate could finally take their places in the coach. The leading coachman climbed up to his perch, and bade the postillions take their places. Then they were off.

Spring was everywhere to be seen as they traveled, and Kate found herself unexpectedly assailed by pangs of homesickness as they passed fields alive with gamboling lambs. But such weakness had been resolutely banished long before they arrived in London late on the following afternoon. The older ladies were by then showing signs of weariness, though the marchioness's *ennui* was due in no small measure to being obliged to endure the gentle, but unending list of Miss Priddy's complaints.

". . . and so many creaks and bumps as there were, dear ma'am! I declare I scarce closed my eyes the entire night for fear of intruders . . . it will be quite wonderful, I am sure, if I do not sustain one of my migraines as a result."

"Poor Priddy. Perhaps a dose of my laudanum would settle you," suggested the marchioness with gentle irony, having learned from Kate that she, too, had spent a restless night, due in no small measure to the snores emanating from Miss Priddy's room, which adjoined her own.

"So kind . . . but, pray do not, I beg of you . . . to deprive your ladyship would be . . . no, no, I will not hear of it . . ." twittered the embarrassed companion, becoming more incoherent with every word.

And so no more was said. But they were all, for different reasons, glad when the outskirts of London were reached.

Kate leaned forward, eager for her first sight of the city about which she had heard and read so much. Dublin had some fine buildings, but everything here was on a grander scale.

She could not have been more fortunate, for the sun was still high, bathing everything in a wonderful golden light. Kate had seen prints of London, but they in no way prepared her for the reality, as each handsome edifice surpassed its fellows. Finally they came in sight of a splendid park. A few flowering trees were still shedding their blossoms, and all were burgeoning into pale green life.

As they approached the park gates, a small procession of fine carriages emerged, with flower petals clinging to them like late snowfall: beyond the carriage windows fashionably dressed ladies could be seen conversing, the younger ones casting flirtatious glances at the peacocks of perfection who rode beside them.

"Hyde Park, my dears," the marchioness told them, amused by Kate's interest, despite her many laughing protestations that such useless frivolities were not for her, and that her come-out would be a complete waste of time and money.

"Oh, how wonderful!" Miss Priddy had revived with miraculous speed upon being told they had almost reached their destination. Like Kate, she had never visited London, had never in fact been beyond High Wycombe. "Everything is so much bigger and grander than I could ever have imagined! And did you see those people? Such elegance of style . . . such refinement of taste. And the build-

ings . . . the carriages . . . Do you not find it all quite
breathtaking, Miss Kate?"

"Quite breathtaking," Kate agreed, amused by
the older woman's fervor. "Indeed, one would have
to be excessively poor-spirited not to be impressed."

Only the marchioness recognized the gentle
irony in her godchild's voice. Many a young girl
would not hesitate to openly mock Priddy's excesses, for she could be exceedingly trying. But
Kate was much too kind-hearted to put her down.

"Oh, you have seen nothing yet, my dears," she
said. "In a few weeks' time, Hyde Park will be
thronged with fashionables of the *haut ton* taking
the Grand Strut, and all vying with one another to
be thought the most stylish. And you, my dear
Kate, will be as fine as any among them. But in the
meantime, we have a great deal to accomplish. Tomorrow, we shall visit Madame Fanchon, who has
had the dressing of me these past—oh, I can't tell
you how many years. Ah," she exclaimed as the
carriage changed pace, "at last, we have arrived."

As she spoke they entered Mount Street, and the
carriages drew to a halt in front of a pleasant well-
appointed house, quite small by comparison with
Kimberley. "Welcome to my London home, Kate. I
hope you will be happy here during your stay."

As if one could be otherwise, thought Kate as the
heavily carved front door opened with almost military precision to disgorge several liveried servants,
the first one coming to let down the steps and open
the carriage door. This accomplished, a butler, resplendent in black and white, moved forward with
majestic tread.

"Grayson, how very nice to see you," said the
marchioness. "I hope you are well?"

"It is kind of your ladyship to ask," he said as he
bowed and assisted her to alight. "I go on very

well, as always. And may I say what a great pleasure it is to have your ladyship with us for the Season. For a while we feared for your health, but his lordship has kept us fully informed. I hope you are now quite recovered?"

"Oh, quite recovered, I thank you. In fact, I'm as fit as a flea," she added briskly. "So there will be no need to cosset me, as I have no doubt my son will have instructed you to do. I daresay he will also have told you to expect Miss Sheridan, who is my godchild. And Miss Priddy . . ." She turned to see Kate encouraging her companion, who was timidly negotiating her way out of the carriage, clutching her portmanteau. "Come along, Priddy. And do put that bag down, my dear. We are not at some inn, now, you know, so you may safely leave everything to the servants."

In a very short space of time, Kate and the marchioness were sitting in front of a blazing fire in the drawing room, enjoying tea and hot buttered muffins. Miss Priddy had declined to join them, expressing a desire to retire to her room, ". . . if your ladyship would have no objection. The coach could not have been more . . . but so long a journey, you know . . . I have the headache, and feel quite dizzy . . . If I might but lie down for a while . . . I am sure I shall be quite recovered by this evening . . ."

The marchioness concealed her relief admirably, merely assuring the poor woman in the warmest tones that she must not think of coming down to dinner.

"It is small wonder that you are worn to a thread, my dear, after so long a journey. And as we shall be dining later here than we do in the country, perhaps you would prefer to have something very light sent up to you on a tray." And as Miss Priddy looked set to be a martyr, "It will be no trouble, I assure you," her ladyship insisted. Thus Miss

Priddy departed, her murmurs of "Too kind, too kind . . ." echoing on the air.

"Oh, dear!" the marchioness whispered, guiltily stifling a trill of laughter. "You don't suppose she guessed how desperately I wished her gone?"

"I'm sure she didn't."

"It's not that I am unsympathetic, but two days' close confinement with Miss Priddy is enough to try the patience of the most exemplary saint. And besides, I am pleased to have you to myself for a while."

"And I, you," said Kate with feeling. "Miss Priddy means so well, but . . ."

"Quite."

Kate broke a companionable silence to say, "This is a lovely big room—so light and airy."

"Thank you, my dear. I confess I am rather fond of the room myself."

Kate chuckled. "It reminds me of our own drawing room back home."

The marchioness's touch was as telling here as it was at Kimberley, for here, too, she had managed to create a complete harmony of comfort and elegance. The silk wall coverings in *eau de nil* made a perfect background for a large Aubusson carpet across which were scattered sofas and chairs of rich brocade. The setting sun cast a golden light over the room as it streamed in through a large window hung with curtains of pale green and gold stripes, looped back with swags.

On either side of the fireplace hung a pair of portraits, the one nearest to her showed a vivacious young woman with dancing eyes as blue as a summer sky, her rich brown curls piled high except for a single curl which had been coaxed to fall to her shoulder, where it lay cushioned in the lace fichou that edged a gown of soft white brocade.

"You have changed very little, Godmother."

Lady St. Clair blushed with pleasure. "It is kind in you to say so, my dear." She chuckled. "Though I fear I could no longer squeeze my figure into that gown. Goodness me, how long ago it all seems!" She sighed, eyeing the picture a trifle wistfully. "I was but seventeen, then, and newly betrothed."

"Mercy!" Kate exclaimed. "At seventeen I'm sure I was still all arms and legs and pimples!" Suddenly restless, she lay aside her napkin and rose, irresistibly drawn to the second picture, which she had seen but fleetingly as she entered.

It was of a man who so markedly resembled the marquess that for a moment she thought it could be no other. He had the same eyebrows and shock of dark hair, and the same piercingly direct blue-black eyes, except that the eyes in the portrait held a gentler expression.

Lady St. Clair watched her surprisingly illuminating profile with interest. At last she said softly, "That is my dear Edward. It was commissioned soon after we were married." And, as if reading her thoughts, "Blaise is very like him, is he not?"

Kate started, as though she had been caught prying. "Yes, indeed," she said, and felt the color creeping into her cheeks.

"A more recent likeness of Edward usually hangs in my room at Kimberley, but the smoke from the fireplace had dimmed its colors and it is away at present being cleaned."

"Does your son live here when he is in London?" Kate asked, unsettled by the thought, for until this moment such a probability had not occurred to her.

"Oh, no, my dear." Kate's blush and the faint note of alarm in her voice had not escaped the marchioness's notice. She continued blandly, "Upon Edward's death, Blaise inherited all the family properties, which include a fine house in Grosvenor

Square, as well as Kimberley and several minor properties . . ."

Kate was not a little shocked that one person should own so much, when others had so little, but her ladyship seemed to take it very much for granted.

"When Edward died, Blaise would have been quite happy for me to occupy a suite of rooms in Grosvenor Square much as I do at Kimberley . . ." She smiled. "But I refused on the grounds that a young married man should not be forever saddled with his mother. So he sold his own house in Brook Street and bought me this charming place." She sighed. "Brook Street must have been so full of happy memories, so perhaps it was for the best in the end. And after Freddie was born, Lucinda came less often to London. Ah, well . . ."

In the small silence that followed, a little ormolu clock on the mantelshelf chimed the hour. The marchioness collected her thoughts and said brightly, "Five o'clock. We usually dine about seven. I have every expectation that Blaise will honor us with his company, if only to assure himself of our safe arrival, so I suppose I had better go to my room to rest for a while." She smiled as Kate's expressive face mirrored her feelings. "I daresay that sounds very tame to you, my dear, so you must feel free to do exactly as you please. Perhaps you would like to take a walk . . . explore a little. If you mention the matter to Grayson, he will arrange for one of the maids to accompany you."

At the door she looked back. "And tomorrow morning I shall send word to Madame Fanchon to expect us later in the day." Her eyes were sparkling with anticipation. "Oh, it is going to be such fun, Kate! I never had a daughter to spoil!"

It was very quiet in the room when the marchioness had gone. Kate walked to the far window.

There seemed to be a stillness in the air, as the sun, preparing to set, cast a warm glow over the empty square. A short walk would be pleasant. She was not used to being so long confined in a carriage as she had been for the past two days.

# Five

The marquess was at that moment about to disarm the voluble Italian fencing master whose premises in Bond Street were the haunt of all who wished to practice the noble art. The only sound in the room was the soft scuffing of stockinged feet on the boards, and the clash of steel against steel as the fencing master counter parried yet again, only to find his blade gathered with a finger-light touch, to be held and swept out of danger. Then, swift as light, his lordship's blade disengaged and shot through to bury its tip in the fencing master's frilled white shirt, just above the heart.

"Very neatly accomplished," murmured the Honorable Gervase Merivale from the depths of a comfortable chair. "If the button had been off, Girelli, you'd be dead meat by now."

"And deservedly so, signor," the Italian enthused, an ingratiating smile creasing his humorous, ugly face. "It is for me a privilege to test my skills against such an artist as 'ees lordship! For I say—me, who knows—one can never tell what 'ee will do next."

"Hear that, Blaise? Girelli regards you as an enigma."

"I do not know what is this enigma, signor," Girelli protested hastily, not wishing to offend his most lucrative client.

The marquess looked up from the task of pulling on his hessians, his smile fleeting as though his mind were elsewhere. "Rest easy, man. Mr. Merivale is merely funning."

"Ah! It ees the English humor, yes?"

"Something like that." Blaise reached for his coat and Girelli, relieved, rushed across to help him on with it, smoothing the fine blue broadcloth, aware as always of the rippling muscles beneath.

"Weston?" queried his friend, putting up his glass, though there was no mistaking the particular touch of genius in the cut of his lordship's coat.

"As you say, Gervase." The marquess eyed his friend sardonically, from the tassels of his gleaming hessions, passing over the yellow calf-clingers with a faint shudder, to come at last to the close-fitting puce coat with padded shoulders and a cravat that was a miracle of complexity. "I observe you continue to patronize that new man."

"Wonderful, ain't he?" Gervase drawled. They left Girelli's and began to walk up Bond Street. "Got a style all his own . . . I do endeavor, whenever possible, to foster new talent."

"And how much do you owe him?"

One eyebrow lifted quizzically. "My dear Blaise, he has gained at least ten new clients on the strength of my recommendation. What more can he wish for?"

"To eat, perhaps?" Blaise suggested. "Speaking of which, why don't you come with me to Mount Street this evening? Mama will have arrived today, and is no doubt expecting me to dine with her."

"Ah, well . . ." Mr. Merivale mused. "Not sure about that . . . a trifle encroaching to turn up uninvited, don't you think? No wish to intrude upon family reunions, y'know."

"Don't be a gudgeon, Gervase. When did you ever intrude? Mama will be delighted to see you.

For some extraordinary reason, she seems to like you."

"She has impeccable taste, your charming Mama."

The marquess threw him a quizzical look. "Also, your presence might be helpful. Mama's godchild will be there, too. You remember, she's the young woman I told you about. Making her come-out."

Mr. Merivale threw him a wary look. "Now look here, Blaise—I'm damned if I'll play the gallant to some unbroken filly in order to dig you out of a hole. Eager *jeune filles* simply ain't my style, as well you know." He shrugged uncomfortably. "Not to put too fine a point on't, I'm not at ease with the petticoat brigade at all until they've passed a certain age."

The marquess laughed shortly. "Oh, Miss Sheridan ain't your usual *jeune fille*. Got some very decided notions of her own. She thinks us a frippery set, and finds the mere notion of being on the catch for a husband degrading."

"Good God! Don't tell me she's a bluestocking! They're more frightening than the Amelia Broughtons of this world! Which reminds me, I haven't yet forgiven you for shooting off and leaving me to the mercy of Amelia Broughton."

The marquess's face darkened. "I thought we had exhausted that subject," he snapped. "I admit that in running for cover as I did I behaved like the greenest Johnnie Raw, leaving you to pick up the pieces. But you have been good enough to accept my apologies on that score, so let that be the end of it. All in all, it has been an incredibly tiresome experience."

"Tiresome don't begin to describe our voluptuous young widow's rage when she learned her Lothario had flown," Mr. Merivale murmured with feeling.

"I was never that, dammit!" Blaise flushed, bit-ing angrily on the words. "Amelia's intrigues are known to all, her affairs are legion—but to my knowledge she has always played by the rules. I had no reason to suppose she wouldn't do so this time. And, by God, I was generous, more generous than she deserved. How was I to know she would turn virtuous on me?"

"Ambition, my boy. Think about it. Broughton—rich, elderly, but a commoner—obligingly pops his clogs, leaving her a fortune but no title. Plenty of young *cicisbeos* eager to pleasure a rich young widow . . . She can pick 'em up and drop 'em at will. Then your eyes light on her, and behold, the lovely Amelia has found her heart's desire—a mar-quess with no encumbrances. Mad as fire, she was, when you decamped! 'Hell hath no fury' wasn't the half of it, I can tell you! Pursued me till I was obliged to flee to Brighton under cover of darkness! Last I heard, she'd taken up with Lingard—you know, weedy young sprig, heir to the old Duke of Tetherington, who's as rich as that Croesus chap-pie . . . and like to drop dead any day now . . ."

But his friend was no longer listening. The mar-quess's attention had been drawn to a young woman just ahead of them in Grosvenor Street. She was unaccompanied, and as they approached, she was accosted by a small and incredibly grubby street urchin with a thatch of black curls. She bent down to speak to him, and after a moment, laughed and pressed something into his hand, and the child ran off.

"You are in luck, Gervase, for, if I am not mis-taken, you are about to make Miss Sheridan's ac-quaintance," he said, increasing his stride, his voice clipped with anger.

"Lord St. Clair, what a coincidence!" Kate ex-claimed as he strode toward her. "Your mother was talking about you earlier. She hopes you will be joining us for dinner. I am sure you'll not be wishing to disappoint her."

"Never mind about dinner," he said abruptly. "That urchin—did you give him money?"

As she looked up at him, puzzled by the abruptness of the question, one flagrantly red curl escaped her bonnet and lay tantalizingly on her brow. The remnants of a smile still lingered in her questioning green eyes as they lifted to his.

"Yes," she said lightly. "A penny only. It was all I had."

His frown lightened, but did not wholly vanish. "Well, that is something to be thankful for, I suppose. But you will be well advised not to do anything so foolish again, Miss Sheridan. The streets are full of such ragamuffins. They make a very handsome living, gulling the naive—"

"Oh, if that is all . . . to be sure, a penny won't get that poor wee mite very far," she returned, her eyes now dangerously bright. "And I will thank you not to call me naive, if you please. I have seen children like Joss many times back home. Sure, Dublin is alive with them."

"Maybe so, but London is not Dublin, ma'am. There are certain codes of conduct to be observed. And while we are on that subject, you appear to have no maid?"

The reproof was implicit in his tone. She faced him, head high, her green eyes very bright. "Lady St. Clair did mention something about asking Grayson for a maid to accompany me, but it hardly seemed necessary, my lord. I had no intention of walking more than a short distance."

"It is always necessary. In London, young ladies never venture out unaccompanied—even for the shortest distance."

"Oh, but that is absurd!"

A discreet cough drew their attention to Mr. Merivale, who had been observing their exchange with considerable interest. Her ladyship's protegée—for it could be no other—was not at all as he had imagined. But Blaise was wearing his most forbidding expression.

"No wish to intrude . . . but, if I might have the pleasure?" he suggested pleasantly.

His lordship swung around, his exasperation held in check as good manners prevailed. "My pardon, Ger. Miss Sheridan, permit me to introduce Gervase Merivale. He's a frippery fellow, but quite harmless."

"Y'r servant, Miss Sheridan." Mr. Merivale made a leg and said in his droll way, "I beg you will not regard my friend's somewhat niggardly encomium . . ."

"Indeed I won't, for I am delighted to make your acquaintance, Mr. Merivale." Kate smiled warmly, offering her hand. "Lady St. Clair has more than once spoken most kindly of you."

"Her ladyship thinks well of everyone, ma'am . . . one of her most charming characteristics, in fact." A lazy smile lurked in his eyes. "Pity her son don't seek to emulate her . . ."

Kate looked from one to the other. Mr. Merivale, with his mincing ways and extraordinary dress, was the epitome of everything she had expected to despise in London society. Had it not been for Lady St. Clair's obvious affection for him, she might have dismissed him as a figure of ridicule, and missed the acuteness of his observation. Even so, the two men were so disparate in every way that she wondered that they would have anything in common. Yet, beneath the chaffing and the drollery, she sensed a true bond of affinity.

She said lightly, "I am not so easily fooled, gentlemen. Only good friends may exchange insults with such ease."

"I had no idea you were such an acute expert in the study of human behavior, Miss Sheridan," the marquess observed dryly.

"Nor am I, sir," came her swift reply. "But, being the eldest girl in a large family, I have long since come to regard such behavior as commonplace."

Mr. Merivale's deceptively sleepy gaze moved from one to the other. "Miss Sheridan's hit, I believe, Blaise. Pinked you, egad. Slipped under y'r guard, neat as a whistle."

"I shall live to fight another day," said his lordship suavely.

Kate looked at Mr. Merivale with new interest. "You are a swordsman, sir?"

"Not I, ma'am." He shuddered delicately. "Deuced dangerous, don't y'know. And exhausting. Leave all that sort of nonsense to Blaise."

"Quite so. But if you can raise a modicum of energy, we will escort Miss Sheridan home."

Kate thought his sarcasm quite uncalled for, but Mr. Merivale seemed to take it all in good part, so it was obviously a kind of game they played—like a charade. "There is no need to trouble yourself, my lord."

"It is no trouble, Miss Sheridan."

Kate detected a note of censure in his smooth tones, and flushed, her chin lifting stubbornly. "Even so, I cannot accept the need. The streets are empty of people. And, if someone were to see me, I refuse to believe that society would shun me for so trivial an offense."

"Triviality has nothing to do with it," the marquess said curtly.

"Not the done thing, d'y'see," murmured Mr. Merivale with one of his sleepy smiles. "Bad *ton*, and all that."

"Oh, really! How absurd!"

"It may very well seem absurd to you, Miss Sheridan," his lordship continued relentlessly, "but if you wish to be accepted in polite society, you must, perforce, obey the rules, however irksome they may seem to you."

Kate flushed. "Then I'm not at all sure I do wish it," she exclaimed impetuously. "For I never heard such a deal of pretentious nonsense."

"Oh, come, dear young lady, you are very hard on us," pleaded Mr. Merivale. "It is but a charade we all play, an' a vastly entertaining one withall. And it hurts no one."

She laughed, then, for it was impossible to maintain her air of indignation in the face of so persuasive an argument. "You make it very difficult for me to cavil, sir, without appearing small-minded."

"And that, I am persuaded, you could never be."

The marquess eyed them quizzically. "When you have stopped tipping the butter boat over one another, might we perhaps proceed to Mount Street?"

Dinner that evening was a surprisingly relaxed and enjoyable event, due in no small measure to Mr. Merivale's presence. The marchioness was delighted to see him, and confided later when she and Kate retired to the drawing room, leaving the gentlemen to their port, that dear Gervase always brought out the best in her son.

"They could not be less alike is so many ways, and yet he has been such a good friend to Blaise. And never more so than during those first terrible weeks and months after Lucinda . . ." She paused, collected herself, and continued, "I have sometimes wondered whether my son would be here now, had Gervase not refused to leave his side until his first tide of grief was spent."

"That cannot have been easy," Kate murmured, having seen his lordship in full tirade. "But one does sense that beneath Mr. Merivale's gentle indolent pose, there lurks a wise and deceptively acute gentleman."

"You are clearly an excellent judge of character, my dear. I just wish . . ." Lady St. Clair paused as if uncertain how best to express her innermost feelings. "No matter. Let us talk of happier things. Our visit to Madame Fanchon, for instance."

At a little after noon on the following day, the marchioness's carriage drew up outside Madame Fanchon's discreetly opulent premises in the vicinity of Henrietta Place, where they were ushered in with a stream of fractured English, of mingled pride and deference, that made Kate wish to laugh, for she suspected that Madame's manner was as contrived as her French accent.

"I beg your ladyship will be seated." Madame led them to a small gilded settee. "Ah, but Ma'moiselle has the coloring, most *magnifique* . . . it will be a joy to have the dressing of her . . ."

For the next hour or more, as she quickly lost all track of time, Kate was bewitched, bemused, and finally spellbound by beautiful materials: everything from the most delicate silks and muslins, lawns and cambrics, to the more serviceable woolens and chintz, and velvets in wonderful jewel-like colors. "Exquisite!" Madame sighed. "It is a fact that white is much favored for the *jeunne filles*, and on mademoiselle white will undoubtedly be superb, but with such hair, such a complexion, to be thus confined would be a travesty!"

Thereafter, one following upon another, seductively soft swatches of material were held against Kate, and discussed with her ladyship as if she were not there.

"I cannot possibly need so many clothes!" There was a note of panic in Kate's frantic whisper to the marchioness, as Madame yet again remembered a particular silk she had in mind for the ma'moiselle, and went in search of it. "Glory be! Poor Pa will be bankrupt, entirely!"

"Nonsense, my dear." The marchioness was complacent, though her eyes sparkled. "I have received very clear instructions from your mama, who knows precisely how many gowns one requires in the course of a Season. And I must tell you that to be seen forever wearing the same one displays a niggardly disposition which would be much frowned upon."

When Madame returned, the silk in question proved to be of a green that exactly matched Kate's eyes, and any lingering resistance melted away.

"Me, I am seldom wrong," Madame declared triumphantly. "It will be *ravissant*!"

And, for once, Kate could not but agree.

# Six

"I should like to give a ball for Kate, Blaise." The marchioness paused, choosing her words with care. "Quite soon—the end of May, I thought."

"As good a time as any," he agreed suavely, "since your sole purpose in bringing Miss Sheridan to London is to launch her into the *ton*."

It was the way he said Kate's name, she thought with a sigh, as if he still disapproved of her. And she had so hoped, even before he left Kimberley, that they were beginning to like one another rather better. Certainly on that first evening in London, the conversation at dinner had been quite stimulating, although that was largely due to the presence of Gervase Merivale, who was the perfect guest. And it was certainly pleasing to observe that Gervase and Kate had got on quite splendidly from the first.

However, Blaise had not called more than once since that first evening, and then on a day when they had been out. She watched him now, prowling the room as if he could not be still.

"Though I could not possibly hold a ball here."

"Quite," he agreed smoothly.

"Of course, Grosvenor Square would be the obvious place." And when he did not immediately answer, she persisted, "You would not mind? If Kate were to make her debut in Grosvenor Square?"

"Mind?" He quirked an eyebrow, though his voice was less than enthusiastic. "My dear Mama, why should I mind? The house is still as much your home as mine, as I never tire of telling you, for all that you choose to be independent."

"Yes, I know, but . . ."

Surely he could not have forgotten? Her own memories of the last time the ballroom had been in use were still vivid, still poignant, despite the years that had passed; memories of the wonderful wedding night ball they had held for Blaise and Lucinda—and how the cream of London Society had been there to see the two of them so in love.

"It was simply that I wondered . . ." She found herself quite stupidly stammering, ". . . the ballroom has been under covers ever since . . ."

He wheeled around, his face a pale mask. "For heaven's sake, Mama. That I haven't as yet chosen to use the ballroom doesn't mean I see it as some kind of sacred shrine, to be forever kept in shrouds."

"No, my dear, of course not." Oh, dear, would the hurting never cease, she thought wretchedly. She had so hoped that by now . . . "It is only . . . I would not want to do anything to arouse painful . . ."

He hurried across the room, his coattails flying, and took her hands, carrying them to his lips. "Mama, forgive me!"

"There is nothing to forgive, Blaise, dear."

"Oh, but there is. I was abominably rude, and not for the first time. See, I have made you cry . . ." He lifted a finger to wipe away a single tear. "It seems that I hurt you constantly . . ."

"No, indeed, what nonsense," she declared stoutly, so that only the veriest tremor betrayed her. "I am just a silly old woman."

"Oh, what a hum!"

"If only . . ."

His long, strong fingers crushed hers. "Don't!" he begged her. "It is useless to wish for what cannot be. I have already traveled that road far longer than sense or sanity dictates. Now I am resolved to be reconciled—truly." His eyes met hers steadily. "Truly," he repeated. "Have your ball, by all means. What better way to banish any lingering ghosts?"

"Well, if you are sure . . ."

"I am sure."

He raised her hands to his lips, then released her and turned away. When next he spoke, it was with a deliberate lightness, though there was a tautness about his shoulders.

"So, where is your protegée this afternoon?"

Pity mingled with relief as the marchioness watched him. But it would not do to let him see.

"Oh, Hetty Melchester invited Kate to one of her afternoon concerts. Sadly, I had the tiniest twinge of a migraine and was obliged to cry off . . ." Lady St. Clair's innocent gaze met her son's quizzical one, for her dislike of all such amateur performances was well known to him.

"I am happy to see you so swiftly recovered."

"Thank you, dear boy," she said, ignoring the gentle sarcasm. "However, it seemed a pity to deprive Kate of an opportunity to meet people. She has met the Melchesters several times, and I had no qualms about sending her in the carriage alone, for she is no shrinking violet. Already she is well able to hold her own in company, without ever putting herself forward unbecomingly."

"A most resourceful young lady, in fact. I hope we may live up to her expectations."

Again the sarcasm was there, accompanied this time by a glint of humor.

"I'm sure I don't know what you mean, Blaise."

"Nothing derogatory, Mama, I assure you. Miss

Sheridan would be the first to appreciate its meaning, having once confessed to me that she would think it—fun, was, I believe, the word she used—to see how we fashionables disport ourselves."

"Kate said that?"

The marchioness's eyes twinkled, even as she felt a stirring of curiosity as to how the two young people came to be on such terms. Could there be more to her son's interest in Kate than he was willing to admit? If so, she would need to tread warily, for fear of putting him on his guard.

"I confess I am not entirely surprised, for Kate is a girl with a great deal of commonsense, and a ready wit. She reminds me quite vividly of her mother, for Elizabeth had a similar dislike of pretension. And although we have as not yet attended anything of a formal nature, I have every expectation that she will aquit herself admirably, whatever the situation."

"She has obviously won your heart, Mama," he said dryly.

"I hope I may not be considered overpartial, Blaise," his mother asserted defensively. "Hetty shares my opinion. She is quite as delighted as I am that her youngest girl, Chloe, and Kate have become friendly, and it pleases me that Kate should have someone near her own age in whom she may confide all her secrets."

"Does Miss Sheridan, then, have secrets?"

The marchioness laughed. "But, of course, my dear. All young girls have secrets. Why, I remember when Elizabeth and I were girls . . ."

"Enough, dear Mama, I beg of you! If you are about to reminisce, I'm off." There was, however, a gleam of humor in his eyes as he retrieved his beaver hat from the table. "Truly, I must go. The horses will be growing restless, and Pogson will give me one of his set-downs . . ."

His mother laughed again, happy to see him at ease once more.

"Oh, what a tarradiddle! You know the poor man worships you. He would not otherwise have tolerated you all these years. There is one small thing, dear Blaise, before you leave. Do you suppose you might have a horse in your stable that would suit Kate? Or, if not, would you be so kind as to procure one? I suspect that riding is something she really misses."

He bent his quizzical gaze upon her. "I trust you do not think to cast me in the role of escort and social mentor to Miss Sheridan, Mama."

"As if I would, my dear," she replied casually. "I hope I know you better than to try."

"Good. Because I warn you, *that* is a horse that *won't* run. However, since you ask it of me, I daresay I can provide your protegée with a suitable mount. Just so long as you don't expect me to dance attendance on her thereafter."

"You have my assurances, Blaise. In any event, I doubt she would accept you in any such guise," his mother answered blandly. "For I doubt it will have escaped your notice that Kate has a highly independent streak. Also, Chloe's cousin, young Stanford, is already much taken with her."

"That young pup!" His blue eyes gleamed. "He doesn't have a brain in his head. He'd never hold her interest for long enough to merit any favors."

"Don't be too sure, my dear. Charles is a very agreeable young man—still a trifle immature, perhaps, but he is the Duke of Walingham's nephew and heir to a sizeable fortune."

"He also has a deplorable seat on a horse, and *that* wouldn't suit your Kate one little bit. She could ride him into the ground without the least effort, and with one arm tied behind her."

"Do you say so?" Lady St. Clair opened wide, innocent eyes. "You are very dismissive, Blaise, but we shall see. Riding isn't everything to a girl, and Kate could do a lot worse. However, Stanford is but one option. I am convinced that after the ball there will be any number of gentlemen anxious to pursue their acquaintance with her."

"I hope you may be right." He smiled and bent to kiss her cheek. "But then, dear Mama, you were ever an optimist."

The genteel strains of a string quartet drifted down from Lady Melchester's salon which faced onto Mount Street. Inside the salon, some twenty people, a high preponderance of ladies among their number, sat on little gilt chairs and sofas, listening with varying degrees of attentiveness as the Bach prelude was followed by an exceedingly thin young man with a violin, who proceeded to give them his tentative adaptation of a Vivaldi sonata.

Kate had never claimed to be more than competent in the realms of musical expertise, but she could at least hold a tune, which was more than could be said for the unfortunate youth.

These reflections were interrupted by Chloe Melchester, a pretty girl with a mass of dark curls confined by a pale blue ribbon that matched her muslin gown, who laid an urgent hand on Kate's arm and indicated a lady in puce whose head had sunk into the lace that adorned her ample chest.

"Lady Bracewell is snoring," she whispered with unholy glee.

"Would that we might be allowed to follow her example," murmured Kate, stifling her own mirth. "At least she is managing to perform quietly, and to rather better effect than this lackless youth."

The violinist's contribution was mercifully short, its conclusion being greeted with a polite patter of applause by all but his mother, who clapped enthusiastically. He was followed by a soprano as immense as the youth was thin, who attempted the impossible in an effort to convince her audience that she was Mozart's pert Cherubino.

The outbreak of conversation as the first part of the program came to a close masked the opening of the door, but the faint draught of air caused Kate to look up, the laughter still lingering in her eyes, to see the marquess with quizzing glass raised, unhurriedly surveying the company until his glance came to rest at length on her.

"Oh, glory!" she whispered, causing her companion to follow the direction of her glance.

"Lud!" Chloe's astonishment equaled her own. "Whatever is *he* doing here? He never attends anything as tame as this! Mama has long since given over asking him."

The marquess, seemingly unperturbed by the amount of interest his arrival was arousing, bowed almost imperceptibly to Kate before strolling across to where plump, pink-cheeked little Lady Melchester sat fanning herself, resplendent in deep blue sateen, much trimmed with lace which also adorned a frivolous cap. She greeted the marquess with teasing affection, and extended a hand to him.

"My dear Blaise, you have come just in time to hand me up—ah, that is better," she exclaimed as he brought her firmly yet gently to her feet and steadied her as she smoothed her skirts. "Though I cannot imagine what has brought you to my trifling entertainment. However, you are very welcome, I'm sure. I had hoped that Brummel would be here to lend consequence to the afternoon, but you will serve almost as well . . ."

"You flatter me, ma'am," he murmured, amused.

"Not at all," she assured him. "To tell the truth, Charles avows the Beau is gambling so heavily these days that he is no longer to be relied upon. It

is a great shame. Of course, I myself believe that he
has never really recovered from his quarrel with
Prinny, though he denies that this is so. However,
that is neither here nor there. I daresay you will
know most people. Your mama's godchild is here—
so sad she could not come herself—and you will
have seen your friend Mr. Merivale over in the corner there with poor Miss Gosporth, doing the polite
. . . such a dear man . . ."

"And Sir Charles?" he quizzed her, having observed her errant husband entering the portals of
White's not ten minutes since.

She tapped him with her fan. "Oh, fie—you must
know that Charles never attends my little afternoons. Not his kind of thing at all—any more than
it is yours—though it is always a pleasure to see
you, as I have told you many times." Her ladyship
eyed him with a shrewdness that belied her tendency to chatter. "So, why are you here, Blaise?"

"Do I have to have a reason, ma'am?"

"Oh, I think so. I have known you since you
were a sprig of a lad, and in all that time I have seldom known you to do anything without good reason."

He was silent a moment, apparently watching
the footmen quietly moving among the guests with
plates of delicacies. When he next spoke, his voice
had a curiously blank quality. "You alarm me,
ma'am. Am I so easy to read?"

"Only by those who care to look beyond the su-
perficial, dear boy," she said in quite a different
tone, and seeing him frown, added, "But there, I
won't tease you anymore. I believe I must rescue
Mr. Merivale. He has performed most nobly, but a
little of Miss Gosporth goes a very long way, and,
polite as he is, I vow his eyes are beginning to glaze
over. You know almost everyone, I believe. And if
tea or chocolate should not be to your taste, a word

in Hebden's ear, an' he will find you something more to your liking."

"You are more kind than I deserve, ma'am." He smiled suddenly and with unfeigned amusement. "Uninvited, as I am . . ."

"Oh, fiddle!" said Lady Melchester, her eyes twinkling conspiratorially in return. "An', should you wish to escape, the concert will resume in about twenty minutes."

It was some little while before Kate and the marquess crossed paths, and in the meantime he was obliged to endure much comment and gentle raillery from friends of his mama's, who were well aware of his dislike of such gatherings.

Mr. Merivale commented in similar vein, having finally been granted his release from the loquacious Miss Gosporth.

"Decided to set a few hearts a'flutter, have we, dear boy?" he murmured, standing back a little and putting up his glass. "You have a new way with your cravat for the occasion, I see. Very fetching. You will have to show me the way of it."

"Not a chance, Gervase. I leave all that sort of nonsense to you."

Gervase accepted the compliment with complacence. "Tell the truth, I'm not quite m'self this afternoon. If I show a tendency to ramble on, pray accept my apologies. You find me suffering from a surfeit of Miss Gosporth. They call Lady Jersey 'Silence,' but poor Miss Gosporth could give dear Sally lessons in nonstop loquaciousness . . ." He sighed. "You may think me poor-spirited, but y'know, doing the polite can be unbelievably exhausting."

"Which is why I seldom frequent such affairs."

"True. So what brings you today?"

The marquess was fast beginning to regret the impulse which had brought him.

"Lady Melchester asked much the same question."

"And?"

"Call it a whim."

Mr. Merivale put up his glass, his keen eyes belying the sleepy drawl. "Known you a long time, Blaise. Never known you succumb to impulse. Feeling a touch under par, are we, dear boy?"

"Not as yet, but if you are minded to be tiresome . . ."

"Ah well." Mr. Merivale lowered his glass and said, almost too casually, "Your mama's protegée, Miss Sheridan, is here this afternoon. Such a charming young lady. Surprisingly knowledgeable about music."

"Really?" The marquess was equally casual. "There would seem to be no end to that young lady's talents . . ."

"Good afternoon, my lord."

Even before he turned, he knew. The Irish lilt was unmistakable. His first thought upon seeing her was that his mama had shown great sense in taking her to La Fanchon. The clear green of her high-waisted silk gown exactly mirrored her eyes, its simple lines giving her slim figure a fluidity that for a moment evoked in him the image of a water nymph—a notion immediately rejected. It was, he told himself, as foolish as it was inaccurate, for there was nothing in the least nymphlike about her.

"Miss Sheridan." He bowed. "An unexpected pleasure. And Miss Chloe, too." The young girl blushed and demurely lowered her eyes. "Y'r servant, ladies."

Kate, unlike her friend, smiled up at him without a hint of shyness or nerves. "I had not expected to see you here, my lord. From something your mama said, I formed the distinct impression that musical afternoons seldom found favor with you."

"Whereas you, so Gervase informs me, are much more appreciative," he replied.

She chuckled, acknowledging his adroitness in avoiding a direct answer. "Yes, indeed. But then, as I'm sure you will allow, appreciation may be achieved in many ways. Chloe and I have been highly entertained thus far, have we not, Chloe?"

Her young friend's reply was somewhat incoherent, leaving Kate to conclude cheerfully, "As you may discover for yourself, my lord, if the second half of the concert mirrors the first. That is, if you mean to stay . . ."

"Sadly, I have a previous commitment." The gleam in his eyes dared her to challenge him. But she—wisely, if disappointingly—resisted the temptation. "I came hoping for a word with Sir Charles, but he is not at home."

"Oh, what a shame!"

"Isn't it?" he agreed suavely. "However, my business will keep." He saw that people were beginning to settle down. "I had better leave, so that you may all take your seats once more. I trust the second half of the concert will give you as much pleasure as the first."

"You are very kind, my lord," Kate said demurely.

He bowed, turned to leave, and as an afterthought, turned back. "I almost forgot, Miss Sheridan. My mother is of the opinion that you are missing your morning rides."

"I surely am."

"Then perhaps you will allow me to provide you with a suitable mount. I doubt Silver would adapt to town conditions . . ."

"No, indeed." They both smiled, causing the others to look at them curiously. "But I would not wish to put you to any trouble, my lord."

"Then I shall call 'round tomorrow morning, and we can perhaps discuss it further."

"You are very kind," she exclaimed.

"Am I? I wonder?" His expression was inscrutable as he once again made his farewells and left.

# Seven

The marchioness took breakfast in her room, and seldom appeared before the middle of the morning. To Kate, who was used to being up and about early, this seemed a shocking waste of time, especially when there were so many places of interest to see. With Ellen, the young maid who had been assigned to her, as her guide, she had formed the habit of taking a brisk walk before breakfast to sharpen her appetite.

There was something quite special about this time of day. Mount Street and beyond lay quite still, if one discounted the occasional tradesman crying his wares, or a maidservant scrubbing away at her steps and polishing brasses. Kate remembered her first visit to a Dublin theater, and thought it was exactly like that moment just before the play began, when a great hush descended on the audience as they waited for the curtains to part.

On the morning following Lady Melchester's concert the air was still chill enough to cloud their breath, but before long the sun would be up, bathing the London streets with golden light. In Balwhinney, she thought, the family would already be sitting down to breakfast. An unexpected surge of homesickness assailed her, and she brushed it resolutely aside.

"A morning for the park, I think," she said with

determined brightness, gathering around her the heavy cloak she had worn to withstand the perils of the Irish sea.

"Yes, miss," Ellen agreed, stifling her shivers, for it beat scrubbing steps an' that, as she'd done often enough in the past, and anyway, Miss Sheridan was a really nice lady—always made you feel like a real person—not like some she'd known.

Mist hung over Hyde Park as they entered through the Stanhope gate. It clung to the tops of the trees, lending a faint surreal stillness to the scene. Ellen shivered. Then, even as she watched, the mist became tinged with gold and everything was bathed in its light.

"Oh, miss! Isn't it beautiful—like magic!"

Kate laughed. "And so it *is* magic, didn't anyone ever tell you? Back home on a morning like this, we say that God has sent his little leprechauns out to paint the trees with gold dust."

"Lordy me!" Ellen exclaimed, big-eyed. "Is that right? An' what are they, them leper . . . what you said?"

"Leprechauns. They're a kind of fairy," Kate said, smiling, "and a right mischievous lot they can be at times."

"My mam says fairies is rubbish. She says only daft people believe in them."

There was a kind of half-yearning, half-defiance in Ellen's voice, as if she wanted to believe, but her mam's word was law. Kate knew she would have to tread carefully.

"Ah, well," she said. "It's maybe only in Ireland that we have such things. You see, Ireland is a magical kind of a country, full of myths and legends, and who's to say what is true or false."

This appeared to satisfy the young maid, and as they turned for home, the last wisps were floating away, the sun was up, and life had already resumed reality in the form of the occasional distant horseman letting rip along the deserted tan.

They were about to turn into Mount Street when a small figure came hurtling across the road into their path. Ellen screamed and caught at the boy's coat, and the cloth ripped apart in her hands. "Look out, Miss! 'e'll rob you blind!"

"He may try, but I have little worth stealing," Kate declared, and in a moment had the boy fast. "Struggle away, my lad, for all the good it will do you. I have twin brothers at home not much older than you, and they never yet got the better of me."

As the boy continued to spit defiance, with shouts of "Gerrof" and "Lemme go!" a burly red-faced man in a once-fashionable topcoat and dusty boots, who had been hard on his heels, came puffing to join them, a riding crop wildly stabbing the air. "Ar! You got 'im, then, ma'am. Jus' you wait, yer little tike . . . an' see if I don't give yer a leatherin' yer won't ferget!"

Hearing these threats, the boy seemed to sag. He clung to Kate's skirts, pushing his head in the folds of her cloak, all bravado gone. "Don' lerrim have me, lady . . ." the muffled voice pleaded. "That Proudy—'e'll kill me, certin sure!"

"Too right, I will . . . an' it no more'n you deserve, yer thievin' little bastard!" The man's eyes were bloodshot beneath a greasy beaver hat. "Gerron outta there, an' take what's comin' to yer, fer the jig's up . . ."

"Let 'im go, miss!" Ellen pleaded in a frightened whisper. "It's best if you do. Urchins like 'im, they're two a penny . . ."

"S'right. Yer maid 'as the truth of it . . ."

"*Please*, lady!" The boy pressed closer, total despair in the muffled plea.

"Give over wingein', yer little scuttler . . . what

would a God-fearin' lady be wantin' wiv the likes
of you?"

The child looked up at last, his eyes big, bloodshot, and scared in his dirty face. And in that moment Kate recognized him, though his former
jaunty air had quite deserted him.

"Joss?"

A puzzled look came into his eyes, then: "You
once give me a penny," he said, his shaky voice
tinged with hope.

"Ha! Which you didn't 'and over," growled the
man, "fer I've not seen no penny." He gave Kate a
sly look. "There's yer proof, ma'am, if proof wus
needed. 'e's a thievin' little tyke, an' he'll feel the
weight of me hand, good and true fer that . . ."

Kate felt the child tremble, and she thought of
Michael and Calum back home, who were little
older than this child, but fit and healthy and full of
innocent mischief.

"You will not touch the boy," she found herself
saying calmly. "In fact, since you think so ill of Joss,
I will buy him off you."

"Miss . . . !"

Ellen's plea was almost a groan. But Kate was
aware of nothing but the man's face, seeing the sly
look that came into his eyes.

"Ah, well now . . . I don't know as 'ow I could
bring meself to sell 'im, missus . . . fer all e's a
reg'lar 'andful at times . . . been mother an' farther
to Joss, I 'ave."

"No, you en't!" Joss cut in. "You only wants me
ter steal for yer . . . *an'* I get beaten somethink 'orri-
ble fer me trouble . . ."

"You shut yer face, or I'll shut it for yer."

"Enough," Kate said, plunging a hand into the
deep pocket of her cloak and bringing out some
coin. "Two shillings, Proudy. It is all I have on me.
You would do well to take it, and cut your losses.

Sad fact though it is for me to contemplate, I'm sure you have other boys to beat. I can do little about them, but at least Joss shall have his chance." He flushed with fury and seemed about to haggle. "Or would you rather I called a constable?" she suggested, with a coolness that belied her inner state. "I'm sure he would be interested in your . . . lay. Is that the word?"

"Doxy!" he spat back at her, and snatched at the coins. "Have 'im, an' I wish yer joy of the little tike. I hopes as 'e robs yer blind . . . which 'e will!"

It was very quiet when the man had gone. Kate's anger subsided as suddenly as it had arisen. Faced with the enormity of what she had done, she wondered what on earth had possessed her, and—more urgently—how she was to proceed. A tug on her cloak made her look down into Joss's filthy, tear-streaked face. He grinned—that cheeky endearing grin she had seen earlier.

"Fanks, lady." His head on one side, he said, "I s'ppose I belongs ter you now?"

"You belong to no one but yourself, Joss," she explained gently. "People have no right in law to own other people, body and soul."

This philosophy didn't seem to have the effect she had hoped for. His face wore a perplexed frown.

"Then where is I ter go, lady?"

"Do you not have anyone, child?"

Joss shrugged. "Me muvver died ages back, an' a baby. That's when the old fellar sold me ter Proudy . . ." His frown deepened. "I fink I 'ad a sister once, but she went away . . . mebbe the old feller sold 'er, an all . . ."

Kate exchanged glances with Ellen, who, though sorry, had probably heard it all before and accepted it with a healthy degree of cynicism. Her glance moved on to Joss, who was watching her.

"Is there no one you can turn to?" she persisted.

This time his shrug had a kind of weary acceptance. "I can go back ter Proudy, I s'pose. E'll give us a good leatherin' fer blowin' the gab on 'im, I 'spect."

"No, you can't do that!" Kate sighed. "You had better come with me until we sort something out."

By the time the marquess arrived, a degree of normality had returned to the house in Mount Street. Even so, he was at once aware of an atmosphere. Grayson, though by far too well trained to exhibit so much as a hint of trouble, seemed very slightly distrait—as though a part of his mind was elsewhere.

"Anything wrong, Grayson?" he asked, frowning as he handed his hat and gloves to a waiting footman, who also seemed a trifle nervous. "My mother quite well, is she?"

"Indeed, yes, my lord. Though her ladyship is not yet down."

"I had not expected her to be. And Miss Sheridan?" The major domo indicated that Miss Sheridan was also well, but the marquess, his senses by now attuned to the atmosphere, saw that he had, as it were, hit the spot. However, he had no desire to embarrass Grayson by pressing him further. "It is Miss Sheridan I have come to see. She is, I believe, expecting me."

"You will find her in the breakfast room, my lord."

"Then I'll go through. No need to announce me, Grayson."

"Very good, my lord." Grayson appeared to be about to say more, then changed his mind and bowed.

The breakfast room was filled with sunlight, its rays slanting in through the window and coming to rest on the room's sole occupant, setting her hair aflame.

"My lord." Kate half-rose, and sat down again. "You are . . . that is, I was not expecting you so early."

"Pray calm yourself, Miss Sheridan," he murmured, more than ever intrigued. "My time is entirely at your disposal. Quite simply, knowing how eager you are to resume your morning rides, I roused myself to make a special effort."

The reassurance appeared to offer her little comfort, though she retained an admirable composure.

"You are very kind. May I give you some coffee?"

"You may, thank you," he said, tossing a pair of leather gauntlets onto the table, before disposing himself in a chair facing her and stretching out his long legs. She passed the cup across the table with a hand that shook slightly.

"Strange," he mused, stirring the contents with the deceptive laziness of a wild animal about to pounce. "From the moment I arrived this morning, I seemed to sense a curious atmosphere—as if everyone were a trifle on edge. Is my imagination playing tricks, or have you noticed it also?"

His words hung in the air for what seemed like an age. Oh, glory, he'll slaughter me, Kate thought, for he'll never understand. But if I don't tell him, he'll hear it anyway—from her ladyship or one of the servants. That is, if he didn't already know. But how could he know? Unless Grayson had told him, which he would not, for Grayson was the very soul of discretion—except that she had stretched that discretion to the very limit.

She cleared her throat. "I think . . . that is, I fear I may be to blame for their odd behavior."

He lifted an eyebrow, but said nothing.

She walked to the window, standing rigidly with her back to him, unaware of how young and vulnerable she appeared. At last she turned and told him, as succinctly as the essential details would allow, what had happened, not looking at him, her voice defensive rather than apologetic. When at last she fell silent, it seemed a very long time before he spoke.

"I suppose it never occurred to you that this villainous creature might resort to violence against you?"

It was the last thing she had expected him to say. And his anger, for he was undoubtedly angry, was a quiet, taut anger that was more unnerving than one of his rages.

"Strangely, it did not. At the time, my concern was solely for the child's fate."

"Of course. Why did I not realize that?" His sarcasm was, as ever, cutting. "And, having bought this unprepossessing scrap of humanity for the princely sum of two shillings, pray, what have you done with him?"

"Well, I first had a word with Mrs. Gilbert . . ." Kate saw his look of mystification. "She is your mother's cook, and a great warm-hearted body she is. It was her suggestion that Joss must at least be given a bath and something to eat before anything was decided. I would have scrubbed him clean myself"—his eyebrow shot up, and she hurried on—"but Ellen said it wasn't seemly, and as she also has young brothers at home . . ." A rueful note entered her voice. "But I'm afraid Joss didn't take at all kindly to the idea, though once he was in clean clothes—the boot boy is much the same size—he cheered up amazingly, and when I last saw him, he was tucking into a large bowl of porridge—"

"And afterward?"

"Well, nothing has been decided . . ."

"He will steal all he can lay hands on and make a bolt for it," concluded the marquess, rocking back on his chair.

"You don't know that . . ."

"I know enough. Has my mother been informed of all this?"

"Not as yet. We thought it best not to trouble her until—"

"*We* thought, Miss Sheridan?"

Kate's chin came up. "Very well. *I* thought it best, and not because I feared she would object. Your mother is a very caring person. However, she would have insisted on coming down to see to matters for herself, and hopefully, as I was about to say, we may already have found a solution."

"You astonish me. So soon?"

Kate refused to be put off by the heavy note of sarcasm. "Ellen thinks her mammy might be willing to take Joss for a small remuneration. She has several boys of her own, and when you have a large family, one more here or there makes little difference."

"You speak from experience, no doubt."

"To some extent, yes," she replied swiftly. "The good thing is that Ellen's family live well away from that evil man Proudy's hunting ground, so Joss would be relatively safe. He is a bright boy, and if he could be taught a trade—"

The marquess brought his chair down with a dull thud. "You have a touching faith, Miss Sheridan, but we shall see who proves to be right in the end—just so long as my mother is not inconvenienced . . ."

"She won't be."

"Good. I shall hold you to that." He stood up. "Then, if you have finished your breakfast, perhaps we may proceed? I left Pogson holding the horses, and they will be growing restless."

"Goodness, yes. Whyever did you not say?" Kate eyed his olive green riding coat, the flawlessly cut breeches, and glanced down at her own simple cotton gown. "I suppose I ought to change this for something more suitable? I do have a grand new riding dress—"

"I think not," he said, sounding suddenly impatient. "Time enough for that if one of my animals takes your fancy."

"Then I will just fetch my cloak and bonnet."

Pogson greeted her with genuine pleasure, and Prancer and Prince pricked up their ears at the sound of her voice. She went to speak to them in her soft strange tongue.

"They remember me," she exclaimed as the marquess assisted her into the curricle.

"How could they forget you," he said dryly.

Kate laughed and settled herself with a sigh of contentment into soft leather that was like silk to the touch. "If the twins were here now, wouldn't they be eaten up with envy to see me riding in such splendor."

The marquess spared her a glance as he took up the reins. Her green eyes sparkled and her skin had a healthy color, and this at an hour when most young women of his acquaintance would still be abed with curtains drawn against the disfiguring perils of sunlight. Used as he was to these women who affected to take such luxury for granted, he found Kate's simple, unaffected pleasure surprisingly refreshing.

A short time later, in his stables, she was even more in her element, moving from one horse to another with exclamations of delight and talking to them in that odd way she had. But he noticed that she kept coming back to a restless, tawny mare with bright eyes and a brow marked with a distinctive blaze. The mare nickered softly as she spoke and there was pride and breeding in every toss of her head.

"She is beautiful."

"And something of a handful," he said, knowing full well that she would favor Mayfly. "But no more so than Silver. Could you handle her in the confines of town traffic, do you think?"

"Oh, yes!" she exclaimed. "I am sure I could, my lord, if you are agreeable!" She lifted a shining face to him. "When may I try her paces?"

That face, in all its youth and eagerness, and, yes, innocence, stirred within him a sensation that he had not felt since . . . that he had resolved never to feel again.

He was silent for so long that Kate began to wonder if he was already regretting his generosity. When at last he spoke, his voice had an edge to it, as though he might already be regretting his generosity.

"Let us say tomorrow morning, early, while the Park is all but deserted."

# *Eight*

Kate went immediately to her godmother on arriving home. She found Lady St. Clair sitting in front of her dressing mirror, dappled in sunlight, a pretty muslin scarf about the shoulders of her blue twill gown, while Bertha dressed her hair.

"How pretty you look, ma'am," she exclaimed. And it was true, for the sun highlighted her godmother's fair curls, which still showed not a trace of gray.

Lady St. Clair laughed. "I fear you flatter me, my dear."

"Indeed I do not, for it's nothing less than the truth. Am I not right, Bertha?"

A grunt was the maid's only reply, and the look she directed at Kate was more than usually dour. But her ladyship merely laughed.

"You see how it is," she said playfully. "Bertha has known me too long to tip the butter boat over me, but I shall accept your kind compliment because it pleases my vanity to do so. And if we are to speak of looks, then I must say that you, my dear, are positively glowing. From which I deduce that Blaise has been able to provide you with a suitable mount."

"Indeed he has, and a darling of a mare she is. I am to try her out tomorrow morning, early."

"What energy you young people have! But I am

very pleased for you. Bertha, dear, do stop fidgeting with my fringe. I shall do very well as I am, so you may arrange my blue muslin cap and go about your business. I am sure Miss Kate will oblige me if there is anything further I require."

"If you say so, madam," said Bertha, disapproval in every nuance of her voice.

When the door had closed behind her, Lady St. Clair bit her lip guiltily, though her eyes twinkled. "Poor Bertha. But she can be very possessive, you know, and a small set-down now and again does her no harm."

Kate knew the time had come to confess. "I fear that this time Bertha may have just cause for her grouchiness, and that any blame must be laid at my door."

"Why, what is this, my dear?" Her ladyship turned to look at Kate, seeing the guilt in her eyes. "How can you possibly have offended Bertha?"

"Well, it isn't just Bertha," Kate said. "I'm afraid the whole house has been a bit topsy-turvey this morning." She plunged into a highly colored account of her early-morning adventure. "Perhaps I should have told you about Joss before I left the house—your son certainly thought I should . . ."

"Blaise knew about the child?"

Her ladyship's eyebrows arched in surprise, and Kate thought her voice sounded rather cool, though she could not be blamed for that, for in the retelling of the sorry tale, her own culpability became ever more clear.

"He . . . seems to have a way of knowing most things, ma'am."

"How clever of you to have noticed," exclaimed the marchioness, momentarily diverted. "It is, in general, one of his less endearing traits, for he has a way of making one feel decidedly uncomfortable if it is something you had rather not have confided to him."

"That may well be so, but I fear that this time he was right," Kate admitted wretchedly. "This is your house, and clearly it was not my place to coerce your servants into accepting, however temporarily, a filthy and unprepossessing child of exceedingly dubious ancestry and morals." She drew breath, to gain fresh courage. "Furthermore, I fear I may have deeply offended Grayson in so doing . . . but you see everything happened so quickly, and I didn't know what else was to be done with Joss. My only consideration at the time had been to get him away from that awful man, but he . . . he sort of attached himself to me thereafter, and refused to be set free, and it seemed that he had inadvertently become my responsibility . . ." By now Kate's wretchedness was apparent. "I couldn't think what to do. It was much too early to disturb you, and finally Ellen suggested that I take him down to Mrs. Gibson, who was quite splendid after she recovered from the shock—though it was clear that she and everyone else thought me quite mad—and then the marquess arrived, and . . ."

To Kate's astonishment, Lady St. Clair began to laugh.

"Oh, you poor child, what a time you have had! I wish I could have been there to witness it all! How very enterprising of you to have tackled such a villainous creature so coolly."

"Yes, but—"

"I think perhaps I had better take a look at this contentious scrap of humanity for myself, don't you? Before anything is decided."

It was a very much subdued Joss who was presently admitted to Lady St. Clair's sunny morning room by an expressionless Grayson, who then proceeded to guard the door, while Ellen kept a tight hold of the child. The boot boy's clothes hung loosely on his thin frame, and his feet, unused to shoes, were clumsy in borrowed boots several sizes too big for him. Poor child, thought Kate with a pang. He looked even more vulnerable with all but the most ingrained layers of dirt removed—as if the scrubbing had succeeded, where Proudy had failed, in robbing him of his spirit.

"Joss," she said, taking him gently but firmly by the arm and leading him forward, "this is Lady St. Clair, who is the owner of this house. Will you not say 'thank you' to her?"

"Why should I?" he muttered truculently. "It wus Mrs. Gibson what give me the food an' all."

Kate was about to remonstrate further when Lady St. Clair, eyes twinkling, said, "How very kind of her. You thanked her, I hope?"

"Yeh—even if the tubbin' were 'er idea, first off." His black curls clung damply above eyes that were as blue and bright and thickly lashed as any girl's, eyes that took on a hint of cunning as they swept the room.

"Don't even think about it, you young rapscallion," said Grayson, who had been watching the boy with an eagle eye.

"I wasn't doin' nothin' 'cept lookin'," Joss protested. "Yer can't be taken up fer lookin'." His innocent gaze returned to the marchioness. "Is this really your ken, lady?"

"My . . . ?" She looked momentarily puzzled, then smiled. "My house, you mean? Yes, it is mine."

"Cor! En't you a lucky 'un."

"I believe I am." Her smile deepened into sympathy. "You have no home or family, I am told. So, what are we to do with you, I wonder?"

The wary look returned. "Yer don't 'ave ter do nuffin', lady. I belongs ter this lady, see." He cocked a thumb in Kate's direction. "Give ol' Proudy two shillin' for me, she did."

Kate looked helplessly at Lady St. Clair, then at Joss. "I have explained that to you more than once, Joss—I didn't buy you, I simply set you free."

He looked back at her, his eyes half reproachful, half defiant. "Then it's back to thievin', I s'ppose. Only this time I'll do fer meself." He grinned suddenly. "It mightn't be so bad at that. Know plenty of fencin' cribs, I does . . . reckon I could make a tidy bit . . ."

"And get caught in no time," Kate said sharply.

"What's it ter you," he came back, quick as a flash, "if you don't want me?"

Kate flashed the marchioness a desperate look. "You could learn a trade?"

"I could fly an' all, if I had wings."

"Don't be insolent, boy," Grayson said in a voice that had been known to make many a young footman quail. "Miss Sheridan has already been kinder to you than you deserve."

"Yeh, well . . ." the boy scuffed his feet.

"And don't do that."

Joss heaved a sigh, and looked up at Kate. "The old feller's right, lady. You 'ave been kind ter me, but it'd be best all 'round now if I wus ter go . . ."

He looked suddenly quaintly old and solemn beyond his years, and Kate felt she couldn't bear it. She glanced at Lady St. Clair, who was also watching the boy.

Ellen was trying to attract Kate's attention. "If y'please, miss . . . m'lady . . ." Encountering a severe glance from Grayson, she bobbed a curtsy.

"Ah, yes, Ellen," said the marchioness. "Miss Sheridan tells me your mother might be willing to give Joss a temporary home?"

"Yes, m'lady. I'd have to ask her, of course, but she's well used to boys, me havin' five brothers, an'

all, though they're mostly growed now . . ." Ellen
blushed. "She'd need a bit fer his keep an' that, but
he'd be well fed and me dad'd find work enough
ter keep him out of mischief. He's a farrier, an'
there's always jobs to be done."

Lady St. Clair looked Joss straight in the eye,
speaking in a voice that Freddie would instantly
recognize. "Well, my lad, what would you say to
that?"

"Dunno." Joss scuffed his feet, which brought an
instant reprimand from Grayson. "I like 'orses.
Might as well give it a go, I s'ppose."

"That is no way to speak to her ladyship, un-
grateful boy," Grayson adjured him.

Lady St. Clair said firmly but not unkindly, "I
think, Grayson, that if you and Mrs. Gibson are
agreeable, Ellen had better go to see her mother this
morning. The sooner this matter can be settled, the
better. Joss, meanwhile, will stay belowstairs. I am
sure you will be able to find sufficient work to occupy him."

"If you say so, ma'am," Grayson said in pained
tones. "Come along, my lad, and look sharpish."

When they had left the room, an awkward silence prevailed, until her ladyship said bracingly,
"Come, my dear, there is no need to fret. It would
seem to be a sensible solution all around. The boy
will have a roof over his head and the chance to
make good."

Kate, who had been staring out of the window,
turned impulsively. "Indeed, you are right, and
well I know it. But I know also that my impulsive-
ness has put everyone to a great deal of inconvenience—"

"Nonsense. It does none of us any harm to
occasionally be shaken out of our complaisance."
She smiled encouragement. "And who knows but
that the child's life will be given quite a new direc-

tion. Now, let us give our minds to more personal matters. About your come-out . . ."

The marquess was admitted by Grayson on the following morning just as the pretty ormolu clock in the hall was striking the half-hour. He looked up to see Kate already on her way downstairs.

"Good morning, my lord."

"Good morning, Miss Sheridan," he said dryly. "You are remarkably prompt."

"You said seven-thirty, I believe, my lord. It may be considered fashionable in London for young ladies to keep their gentlemen waiting, but I am used to being about early."

He watched her come down the last few steps, the skirt of her riding dress—clearly another of Madame Fanchon's creations—trailing behind her. The dress was fashioned of bronze-green cloth, embellished in military fashion with black braiding, its high collar edged with lace. A dashing black hat, also braided, echoed the military theme, being reminiscent of a shako even to its neat brim and tuft of feathers.

"Very fetching," he murmured.

"Thank you, my lord," she replied cordially, her riding whip tucked under her arm as she pulled on a pair of soft tan leather gloves. "I am rather taken with it myself. I have never worn anything half so fine."

Pogson awaited them outside, together with his own placid horse, Mayfly, and a beautiful restive bay. Kate greeted him with a happy lack of condescension before turning her attention to Mayfly, who nickered softly and shook her silky mane.

"She remembers you, Miss," said Pogson. "Bright as a button, that one is."

"I could see that at first glance."

"Are you quite ready, Miss Sheridan?" The marquess had come up behind them.

"Yes, my lord. Ready and eager."

Almost before she had finished speaking, he was tossing her up into the saddle. Mayfly jinked and backed nervily. Kate heard Pogson call: "Easy, now, Miss Sheridan. Gentle her an' she'll be fine." But, hampered as he was with the other horses, he could do no more. At the same time the marquess reached out a hand to seize the bridle. Kate brushed it aside and leaned forward to whisper in the mare's wildly pricked ear, easing her around, smoothing her mane, and almost at once, she quietened and stood quite still.

"You handled that well."

His compliment was abrupt, even a trifle grudging, but Kate guessed he was a little piqued that she had managed without him, and was prepared to be magnanimous. "It's just high spirits," she said. "Sure, there isn't an ounce of malice in her. Once she has the fidgets out of her legs, she'll be as biddable as a lamb."

"Right, then we'll be off," he said, mounting his own horse, and leaving Pogson to follow.

"That young lady's a match for you, right enough, m'lord," the groom muttered to himself. "And about time, too."

They walked through the empty streets at a decorous pace, but once within the Park gates, the marquess suggested they might safely canter as the place seemed equally deserted. It had the makings of another beautiful morning, with the mist rolling away to reveal a sky streaked with gold as the sun rose above the trees.

"Mayfly moves beautifully," Kate exclaimed, running a hand down the mare's neck. "I only wish I might really let her out."

He glanced about him, and seeing no one in

sight, said that a short gallop could do no harm.
Soon they were flying down the tan, neck and neck,
until a distant rider came into view.

"Enough," cried his lordship, and they slowed
again to a canter.

"That was wonderful!" Kate exclaimed breath-
lessly, running a soothing hand down the mare's
neck. "You can have no idea how much I have
missed my morning ride. May we do this again
soon?"

He glanced across at her. The exercise had
brought the blood to her cheeks and her eyes were
liquid-bright and filled with laughter as she turned
to him. And something stirred in him that he had
resolved never to feel again.

"Perhaps. Though it is only permissible to gallop
at this time, when the Park is deserted. Try it in the
afternoon and you will be classed as a hoyden."

"Oh, really!"

"Yes, really. I do not jest in such matters."

His voice sounded abrupt, almost curt. Perhaps,
she thought, he was out of breath. Or perhaps he
simply did not wish to become in any way responsible for her.

"I'm sorry," she said quickly. "You are probably
much too busy and too much in demand to waste
your time playing escort to me. I daresay Charlie
Stanford will oblige, if I ask him."

"Are you then on such familiar terms with Stanford?" he asked curtly, not a little piqued.

"I don't know about familiar, but in general I
find him a most agreeable young man—a trifle immature, perhaps, but great fun. He reminds me a
little of Kit." Her voice took on an unconsciously
wistful note.

"Have you heard from your brother recently?"
he asked abruptly, as they turned to retrace their
steps at a more decorous canter.

"No. But then he was ever a terrible correspondent. And it is possible that my parents will have heard from him." This thought filled her even more with homesickness. To alleviate it, she said overbrightly, "I believe you are to host my come-out, my lord?"

He threw her a highly quizzical look, which found echo in his gentle sarcasm. "Oh, surely not, Miss Sheridan. I am more than willing to put the house at my mother's disposal for the great event, but, as for *hosting* your come-out—to cast me in such a role would be inappropriate, not to say a little nonsensical, don't you think?"

Such a withering dismissal of the occasion, which, in spite of all her reservations, had begun to excite her, had the effect of making Kate's pleasure seem like the triumph of self-indulgence over commonsense. Even so, the degree of disappointment she felt surprised her, though she would die rather than let him see it. Nevertheless, her laughter had a brittle edge that set Mayfly caracoling and she was obliged to bring the restive mare under control before speaking her mind.

"Of course it is nonsensical. Have I not already made my own opinion clear to you on that score? But it is a harmless nonsense which will certainly give your mother much pleasure. She quite naturally wishes to create a stir in order to do her best by me, standing as she does in place of my mother, and I would not for the world disappoint either of them." She threw him a challenging look. "Furthermore, to be honest, I am already finding life much more enjoyable than I had expected. However, since you clearly find the whole affair beneath your touch, I would not think of causing you one moment of inconvenience."

Impertinent baggage, he fumed inwardly as they

rode on in silence, until a shout and a pounding of hooves brought Charles Stanford abreast of them.

"It is you, Kate!" he cried, reining in beside her. "How splendid! I thought I wasn't mistaken, though I hadn't expected to find you abroad so early. My cousins are such sluggards—seldom even awake at this hour!"

"That is exactly the kind of remark my brother might make, Charlie," she reproved him, laughing. "And as such, I shall ignore it." She was aware of an oppressive silence on her other side. "I've no doubt you are already acquainted with Lord St. Clair, so I need not introduce you."

"No, indeed," he replied, overeagerly, for he was very much in awe of this, one of the prime leaders of fashion. "Good morning, my lord. A perfect morning for riding."

A curt nod was his only answer.

"Lord St. Clair has loaned me this beautiful mare, who can go like the wind," Kate continued. "Is it not kind of him?"

"Monstrous kind. Good judge, too, for you grace one another, if I may be permitted to say so . . ." He blushed. "Saw you earlier, don't y'know. You ride surprisingly well . . ."

"Thank you," she said with a dryness that quite escaped him. "It was certainly invigorating." Out of the corner of her eye, Kate saw that the marquess was growing restless, and feared that he might at any moment make one of his cutting remarks. "But it is time I returned to Mount Street, or Lady St. Clair will begin to wonder what has happened to me. Shall we see you this evening at Lady Bridgewater's soiree?"

"Oh, I should say so! Looking forward to it," enthused Charlie, who avoided all such insipid affairs like the plague and had been meaning to go to White's. He doffed his hat to each in turn and, dig-

ging his heels into the horse's side, hauled on the
reins to drag the animal around and galloped back
the way he had come.

"Cow-handed," observed the marquess with a
sardonic twist to his mouth.

Kate laughed. "True. But then, I have observed
that young men frequently are. Perhaps it is their
way of showing off—of proclaiming their man-
hood."

"That is a very profound observation."

"It comes of growing up with brothers. But
there's no real harm in Charlie."

"Except that he is still wet behind the ears and
hopelessly infatuated. I hope you mean to let him
down lightly."

"Oh, I believe Charlie and I understand one another very well," she replied equably, urging
Mayfly into a gentle canter.

# Nine

As the evening of her come-out approached, Kate began to feel an excess of nerves quite foreign to her. It was not the event itself, she told herself resolutely, so much as its venue. She had, of course, seen the house in Grosvenor Square many times from the outside, but nothing in her fertile imagination came close to preparing her for the elegance within as Jameson, the stately butler, admitted them for the first time and expressed his pleasure upon seeing her ladyship.

"Thank you, Jameson." Her eyes twinkled as she introduced Kate. "I daresay you may become quite tired of seeing us before long, with so many details to be finalized."

"Not so, my lady," he replied gravely. "You could never be anything less than welcome. Miss Sheridan, also." He bowed his head in Kate's direction with a solemnity that made her want to laugh, though she responded with equal gravity.

"As the ball is now less than two weeks away," her ladyship continued, "I thought it might be as well for Miss Sheridan to familiarize herself with the house."

"Quite so, my lady. I have arranged for tea to be laid out in the blue drawing room, if you would care to go up. I hope that you and the young lady will find all the preparations so far to your liking . . ."

"I am sure we will, Jameson, for you are quite incomparable in dealing with such matters. Did his lordship tell you that we are expecting well over a hundred guests? Quite like the old days." She sighed. "Oh, goodness me, such times we had, did we not? The balls . . . the routs . . . Venetian breakfasts . . . !"

"We did indeed, my lady." Jameson's voice betrayed him more than he knew. "And you may be sure that everything shall be as it was then for Miss Sheridan's ball. The servants are to make a start on the ballroom this very day . . ." He hesitated before concluding, "If I may be permitted to say so, my lady, it will be good to see the house come alive again."

Lady St. Clair longed to quiz him about her son's present state, but knew that it would embarrass him greatly.

"Quite so," she said briskly. "Now, tea, I think. Kate . . . ?"

She turned, and was amused to find her goddaughter quite lost in contemplation, her awed gaze traveling around the entrance hall where six pillars soared up from a pale marble floor to support the ceiling with its domed centerpiece exquisitely coffered and picked out in gold, the overall effect giving an impression of air and light and space.

"Robert Adam designed much of the house for Edward," she explained. "I believe he was always particularly proud of this hall."

"It is very beautiful." Kate breathed the words with a kind of reverence mingled with a strong determination not to allow herself to be overimpressed.

Lady St. Clair laughed. "But perhaps a trifle ostentatious?" she suggested. "I confess I have always thought so myself, though I would never have admitted as much to Edward."

The inner hall was more to Kate's liking. The marble was carried through, but here there was more restraint in its decoration and in the graceful staircase curving toward the upper floor. Even so, she was moved to remark amusedly, "But all this grandeur for one person—it's a terrible waste!"

And then felt herself blushing a fiery red as she saw the marquess coming slowly down the staircase. He must have heard—and the butler, too, she suspected, for he was staring at a point beyond her head, looking as though he had a nasty smell under his nose. Well—her chin lifted—it was said now, and she wouldn't take it back, for every word was true enough.

"Ah, Blaise," said the marchioness, as though nothing untoward had happened. "There you are. I hope you mean to take tea with us."

"Of course, my dear." He raised her hand to his lips. "It is why I am here."

"And then you may escort Kate on a tour of the house," she continued as they made their way up the staircase to a very large, sumptuous—and, Kate thought, very un-lived-in—drawing room, in spite of the huge fire crackling merrily in the grate of an overembellished marble chimneypiece. "She will need to know her way around."

"If you say so, Mama," he agreed with an inscrutable lift of one eyebrow as he settled her into a chair. "And if Miss Sheridan wishes it."

"The house is yours, sir," Kate replied swiftly. "It should be as you wish."

Lady St. Clair looked from one to the other in exasperation.

"What *I* wish, is that you would both stop behaving like children. All this polite formality is driving me to distraction."

His eyes met Kate's, and found them very green, very bright and challenging, her cheeks becomingly flushed. And for a moment, as their glances locked, her expression seemed to change, to be questioning him—and he felt a curious sense of unreality, as if a part of him he had thought dead was struggling painfully back into life. And with the sensation came panic, a tightness in his chest, for he had been down that path before and would not go again ...

It was Kate who broke the spell—dragging herself back to reality, mortified and embarrassed by the way her imagination had, however briefly, taken a quite extraordinary and un-looked-for direction. Her cheeks grew warm. How could she have entertained such thoughts, for even a moment? Had anything in her manner betrayed her? If so, if only for her own pride's sake, it was up to her to disabuse him of any such nonsensical notions.

She forced a laugh, and to her surprise it sounded entirely spontaneous.

"Your mother has the right of it, my lord. If my two young spalpeens of brothers, Michael and Calum, had carried on the way we've been doing, my mother would have boxed their ears and sent them to bed without supper."

For a moment Kate thought she had made bad worse. And then, to her surprise, he smiled, a smile tinged with genuine humor that made him seem suddenly years younger.

"I doubt my mother would go that far, but perhaps it would be wiser not to tempt providence."

"That is much better," said the marchioness approvingly. "And while we are about it, Blaise, can we not have an end to all this 'my lord' and 'Miss Sheridan' nonsense? Such formality is really quite nonsensical in the circumstances. Kate is my god-daughter, which must make her practically one of the family."

"A nice distinction, Mama, and one that had not until now occurred to me." He turned quizzically to Kate. "What does the young lady have to say to it?"

She could feel her cheeks growing warm under his mocking gaze. "Oh, it is all one to me, my lord," she said loftily. "At home we are seldom troubled by such niceties, so if it pleases you to call me by my given name, you are very welcome to do so."

"Then Kate it shall be, and you will call me Blaise."

She felt certain he was hoping to discompose her, and was resolved that he should not succeed. "Very well. Blaise."

"That is much better," said the marchioness. "It is bad enough to have Priddy forever in a twitter, without you forever being on the verge of coming to cuffs."

"Miss Priddy is not indisposed, I trust?"

Her eyes twinkled as she detected an ill-disguised note of hopeful expectation in his voice. "Dear me, no. But poor Priddy is so much in awe of you that she was quite overwhelmed at the mere thought of entering the hallowed portals of Hale House and expressed an earnest desire that she be allowed to visit the British Museum instead."

"Would that they might keep her as an example of one of life's curiosities."

"Blaise! That is not worthy of you," the marchioness reproached him, trying not to laugh. "I only hope I may persuade her to come to the ball. And if she does come, I trust you will endeavor to put her at ease."

"Why not? We seem to be in the business of collecting oddities. How does your young pickpocket fair, Kate?"

"Very well, as it happens," she returned equably. "Ellen's father reckons he has a natural affinity with horses."

"Then let us hope he eschews old habits and settles to his new calling. There will then be one villain less in the world."

The entrance of several footmen bearing trays at that moment gave their thoughts a new direction, and afterward Kate was treated to a tour of Hale House which left her head in more of a spin than ever. It was not as large as Kimberley, but in some ways it was more imposing and less of a home, with gilded salons—some large, some intimate—and an oak-lined library that caused her to exclaim, "Glory, wouldn't my father die a happy man with so many books to browse among!" making her companion laugh aloud. He should laugh more often, she thought, for it changed his whole personality, making him seem years younger.

Finally, they reached the entrance to the ballroom, where mirrors adorned the walls, reflecting an army of servants who worked like beavers, sweeping and polishing. A shaft of sunlight pierced one of the newly washed and burnished crystal chandeliers, sending out shards of rainbow brilliance. Dazzled and dazed, her last lingering doubts about her debut melted away.

"I have never seen a more beautiful room," she said, sighing dreamily, and when he did not answer, turned to find him totally changed, white-faced, his jaw clenched. But it was his eyes that disturbed her most. She had never witnessed such raw pain in anyone.

"My lord?" It was as if she had not spoken. "My lord?"

He heard nothing but the buzz of conversation;

saw only the hundreds of candles glittering in the chandeliers, and the room filled with people in all their wedding finery, all laughing and talking . . . saw them part to reveal a slender girl who came running toward him, a creature of light and air, wearing a cream silk gown with roses nestling at her breast and more roses in her dark cloud of hair, her blue eyes laughing . . . then the shimmering crowds melted away, and she was reaching out her hands to him . . .

"Blaise!"

The urgent voice finally penetrated his consciousness, and the scene fragmented into a thousand pieces. Someone was touching his arm, and he flinched.

"Are you unwell?"

He threw back his head and drew a deep painful breath, his voice, the voice of a stranger. "No, Miss Sheridan. I am not unwell. Merely laying a few ghosts."

He turned unsteadily and walked out of the room, and then paused, as if uncertain which way to go.

His pallor alarmed Kate, and she knew she must do something. There was a small sofa placed against the wall a few yards down the corridor. "Please, my lord, will you not rest for a few minutes?" she suggested, laying a hand lightly on his arm.

"Don't nanny me, Miss Sheridan. I am not Freddie."

"No, my lord." Though you look exactly like your son at this very minute, she thought. "However, it is what my father would suggest, were he here. You will surely not wish to return to your mother in your present state, white-faced and looking as though you had seen a ghost."

The moment the words were out, she wished

them unsaid, for he clearly *had* seen a ghost, or as
near as, and she did not need to be told whose
spirit still haunted that room.

"I'm sorry," she said quietly. "Such frankness
was impertinent in me—and insensitive."

He swung around to look her full in the face, and
she saw that he was already less pale, though his
eyes still burned a little wildly.

"What an odd girl you are," he said abruptly.
"Come. My mother will be wondering what is taking us so long." They retraced their steps in silence.
Only as they approached the drawing room once
more did he once again pause. "I must ask you not
mention my momentary . . . indisposition. She will
only worry."

"It would not have occurred to me to do so, my
lord."

"What an odd girl you are." He repeated, smiling
with a suddenness that took her breath away. "And
it is Blaise," he corrected her dryly. "We are not
doing very well, are we, Kate? But I daresay we
shall grow used to it in time."

That evening in Drummonds, a small gaming
house just off St. James's, in a silence broken only
by the rattle of dice, Mr. Merivale stood among several onlookers and watched his friend with veiled
concern. There was an air of tension among the five
men at the table, which stood in a pool of light surrounded by deep shadows. The flaring candlelight
accentuated Blaise's pallor, and there was a reck-
lessness about his play that Mr. Merivale hadn't
seen since those terrible months following Lucinda's death. His cravat was loosened, he was well
into his second bottle of claret, and a small pile of
gold and paper lay before him.

As if aware of Mr. Merivale's thoughts, the marquess looked up suddenly, and frowned. "What,

you here, Gervase? Thought you were promised to
Fenwick for the evening."

"So I was, Blaise, but he's laid up with the gout."
Mr. Merivale paused, not wishing to reveal that he
had met Melchester, who had commented on having see the marquess entering the club, known for
its reckless play.

"Thought he was over all that nonsense," Melchester had said gruffly. "Don't like to see a decent
fellow like St. Clair frequenting such dens."

"No more do I," agreed Mr. Merivale thoughtfully.

Now, looking into his friend's bloodshot eyes
was like turning back the clock. And his heart sank.

"Come away, Blaise," he said quietly. "This is no
place for you."

"Can't leave now, Gervase," he drawled, without
looking up. "On a winning run, d'ye see."

"Your mother would be distressed, were she to
learn you were here."

The marquess lounged back, his fingers curled
loosely around the stem of his wineglass, his eyes
mocking. "And you would go tattling to her, would
you?"

"For friendship's sake I will forget you said that,
Blaise," Mr. Merivale said quietly.

"Very noble!"

In the silence that followed, several disgruntled
voices urged him to throw the dice. He threw a
main of seven—and lost. When he looked up, Gervase had gone.

Much later, he left the club and walked with the
careful tread of a drunken man toward a certain
house in Half Moon Street where he pulled on the
bell until a maidservant came hurrying in nightcap
and voluminous shift, a lamp held high.

"M'lord!" she exclaimed nervously. "My mistress
is long abed."

"Then wake her, Nellie. She has no business to sleep when I have need of her."

A sound above made them look up. A young woman with a cloud of dark hair cascading onto her shoulders was leaning over the bannister. "Blaise—it's never you!" A husky laugh floated down. "How like you, after all this time, to turn up in the middle of the night! And drunk, by the sound of it."

"Devilish drunk," he agreed, enunciating carefully. "And in need of comfort."

"Then you had better come up, my lord."

# *Ten*

Kate awoke early, and was momentarily disconcerted to find herself in a strange bed, but as her eyes adjusted to the darkness and a room filled with unfamiliar shapes, she remembered that she was at the house in Grosvenor Square, and today was her big day.

In spite of all her avowed protestations about the absurdity of curtsying to London's fashionables, Kate had found herself succumbing to occasional waves of nervous excitement as the day drew near.

This was in part due to Miss Priddy; as the marchioness had observed drolly, one might be forgiven for believing that it was Priddy's come-out, so full of nerves had her companion become as the day drew near, lest her appearance or demeanor should in any way fall short of what might be expected.

"I would not for the world let your ladyship down in front of all your grand guests," she had reiterated only yesterday as they prepared to leave Mount Street. "Perhaps if I were to stay here quite quietly? You must not think I should feel in the least hurt or deprived . . . though naturally, I would be disappointed not to see dear Kate in all her finery . . ."

"Which you will do, dear Priddy, if only you will refrain from harboring such nonsensical notions," said her ladyship briskly. "It is all arranged. A fine thing it would be, I'm sure, if we were to leave you here alone to mope."

And Kate had swiftly added her own assurances that it would disappoint her greatly if Miss Priddy were not present.

"Dear child! So kind . . ." murmured the little companion, clasping her damp handkerchief and raising it once more to dab at her eyes.

Now the day had come and light was squeezing through a chink in the heavy brocade curtains, pearly bright with the promise of a perfect day to come, and highlighting the cover that shrouded the gown Kate would wear that evening against the slightest speck of dirt. It was of palest *eau de nil* silk, very simply cut to emphasize her slim figure. Tiny pale pink silk roses adorned the neckline and were repeated around the hem.

Kate's heart skipped a beat, then she sat up, chiding herself for giving way to nerves for even a moment. It was an occasion to be enjoyed, and enjoy it she would, no matter what.

She rose and padded across to peer at the little clock on the mantel shelf. It wanted but a few minutes to seven o'clock. She woke Ellen, who was in a small adjoining room, and in no time at all, they were dressed and making their way cautiously down the elegantly curving staircase in a silence in which every rustle of skirts seemed to echo like distant thunder.

As they reached the hall, a very young footman appeared from nowhere. Still very new to the job, the words of Mr. Jameson echoed in his ears. *"Self-effacement combined with anticipation, my boy. Do your work well, and you will be accepted as a part of the furnishings, always there when necessary to cater for the well-being of his lordship and his guests."* Not quite sure as yet how this might be achieved, he now bowed very low and diffidently inquired if he might be of some assistance.

Kate smiled encouragingly at him. "Thank you. Perhaps you could open the door for us. We would like to take our usual morning walk."

The footman's mouth dropped open and was quickly closed again. Young ladies, so he had heard—his own experience being woefully lacking in such matters—seldom left their rooms much before midday. And nothing in Mr. Jameson's instructions had made mention of guests being so friendly and forthcoming, or how he should respond to it.

"Certainly, miss," he said, and, using his initiative so as not to appear unversed in the ways of the gentry, hurried to the door and held it open for them.

"Thank you," she said, still smiling. "What is your name?"

He blushed. "Henry, miss."

"We shall be back quite soon, Henry."

"Very good, miss. The porter should be on the door to let you in."

They had scarcely negotiated the steps when a hack stopped outside to disgorge its passenger, an incongruous figure for such an hour, disheveled and still attired in evening clothes, his cravat carelessly tied. The marquess, for it was no other, paused as if stunned, glaring at them out of bloodshot eyes, then bowed, uttered a curt "Good morning," and hurried up the steps.

"Did you see the state of 'is lordship, Miss Sheridan? Still in 'is swell evenin' clothes, 'e was." Ellen giggled. "Been with some light-o-love, like as not. It wouldn't be the first time. You should hear what they've been sayin' belowstairs about 'im returnin' to 'is old ways . . ."

"Be silent, Ellen!" Kate was quite unreasonably angry. "You shouldn't listen to idle gossip. And you will on no account mention having seen his lordship to anyone—not anyone, do you understand?"

"Yes, miss, o'course, miss," Ellen said, though reluctantly, for it would have made a grand story, and there'd be no keepin' it quiet for long—all gossip found its way belowstairs in time. Her disappointment was also tinged with curiosity. It wasn't like Miss Sheridan to speak so sharp. Ellen had occasionally wondered if she wasn't a bit sweet on his lordship, not that it was any of her business.

Kate, lost in her own thoughts, was deeply concerned at how dreadful the marquess had looked—so pale and drawn. She had seen very little of him since that incident in the ballroom not two weeks since, but Chloe had told her in confidence that she had overheard both her father and Charlie discussing him recently—forever in his cups, Charlie had said, and gambling recklessly. "*Back to the bad old days*," had been Lord Melchester's sad comment.

And a recent conversation between Kate and Mr. Merivale at a small informal rout which Kate had attended with her godmother, though couched in discreet language, had seemed to confirm her worst fears.

Mr. Merivale, resplendent in a wine-colored coat cut to fit his slim figure to an inch, and with a complex cravat supporting high collar points, was pleasant and courteous as always, complimenting her on her gown, which was of pale amber over an ivory slip. Yet she could not help but notice a certain coolness in Mr. Merivale's manner when his lordship's name came up in the conversation. And when he hinted that he might find himself unable to attend her ball, and the dinner preceding it, she knew that something was amiss.

"But you have already promised to be there!" she

exclaimed, drawing him aside. "And I am counting on you for support." Her eyes were very bright, very green, as they widened in realization. "This is to do with Blaise, is it not? You surely have not quarreled?" she demanded, frank as ever.

Mr. Merivale's smile, though perfectly polite, had a distant look that discouraged comment. "Nothing of the kind, ma'am, I assure you. One does not quarrel with Blaise."

"I cannot imagine you quarreling with anyone," she said with a spontaneity that brought a faint smile. "Besides, you are his friend—almost his only true friend, I would guess."

"Why, so I had supposed." The smile became rueful. "At school together, don't y'know . . . like brothers. But he occasionally has a way of making friendship deuced difficult."

"Which I suspect he has been doing recently." Kate uttered a little sigh of exasperation. "Honestly, if he were my brother, I would hit him," she said, so vehemently that Mr. Merivale smiled his familiar sleepy smile.

"I'd give a monkey to see his face, an' you did."

She smiled back, but it was a troubled smile. "Except that if his present behavior does indeed give you cause for concern, I fear I may be partly to blame." She saw his eyebrow quirk and swiftly told him how strangely the marquess had behaved while showing her over the house. "He had been almost affable until we reached the ballroom, when he suddenly fell silent. Oh, Mr. Merivale, if you had but seen him . . . the pain-wracked look in his eyes . . . it was quite unnerving. I scarcely knew what to do for the best. But within minutes he had recovered and brushed away my concerns quite tersely." Her words hung in the air.

"Interesting . . ." Mr. Merivale seemed to be choosing his words with care. "Difficult situation, y'see. Not altogether clear how much you know, ma'am . . ."

"Lady St. Clair told me about Lucinda, if that's what you mean, so I know how very much in love they were . . . and how distressed he was when she died . . . cutting himself off from all he cared for . . ." Kate met his eyes. "And the thought did cross my mind . . . their wedding celebrations were held in that ballroom, were they not?"

Mr. Merivale nodded. "Been closed up since her death, d'ye see. Never seen a man so distraught. There were times when I feared for his sanity, if not his life . . ."

"Then it is as I suspected," Kate exclaimed, her face more expressive than she knew. "Oh, what a coil! Except that her ladyship assured me Blaise had been quite adamant that the ballroom should be opened up and used . . . though now I recall, she seemed a little troubled as she said it. I should have realized what it would mean to him . . . the memories . . . Oh, how I wish I had known!"

He had looked at her strangely. "Pray, do not distress yourself, Miss Sheridan. Case of opening old wounds, d'ye see, but Blaise will come about, never fear."

"I do hope so. But it makes your presence all the more necessary, don't you see?" she had pleaded with him. "He will need true friends to see him through, and I am relying on you to lend your support. Please say you will not let me down."

"Deeply touched, ma'am." Mr. Merivale's eyes twinkled. "How can I refuse without appearing ungallant?"

She wondered now if Mr. Merivale had already known the full extent of the marquess's slide back into his old ways. Discretion would have prohibited his saying anything, but on reflection, and having brothers of her own, it seemed likely that he did know, and that they had had words, which had led to a coolness between them.

However, there was no time to brood on such fine points. She returned from her walk to find an army of shirt-sleeved servants in baize aprons and leather breeches already busy erecting an awning from the house, across the flags to the road, while others laid a crimson carpet down the steps beneath it. Soon Grosvenor Square was alive with sound as their good-natured arguments mingled with the whistling of tradesmen and the rattle of their carts.

The time sped past, and the doorbell was never still. Later, she sat opposite Lady St. Clair on one of the fine brocaded couches in the blue drawing room, surveying a pile of letters and packages on the little table before her, not knowing quite where to begin. And then she spied one bearing Kit's flourishing script, and seized upon it.

"Oh, how clever of him to have remembered, though I suspect Mama reminded him, such a scatterbrain as he is!" she cried, scanning the words that tumbled onto the page just as though he were speaking them aloud. "He appears to be having a wonderful time, hunting and dancing—not a word of Bonaparte or the possibility of any fighting!" She laid it aside to digest later and fell to opening the rest.

So many prettily worded notes, small gifts, and bouquets of flowers were delivered throughout the day from friends of Lady St. Clair, many of whom Kate had met, for the knocker had scarcely been still during the few weeks since their arrival in town.

"How kind people are," Kate said, as small ripples of excitement began to mount inside her. "See, this lace handkerchief is from Lady Jersey . . . and such a pretty little pearl ring from dear Lady Melchester . . ."

Best of all, a small parcel had arrived from Kate's mother. As she opened it, notes from each of her brothers and sisters fell out, full of the family's thoughts and wishes for her special day. And a long letter from her mother. *How I wish we could be with you, my darling, but perhaps this trifling gift may keep us in your thoughts. It was your father's gift to me when I made my debut. It cost him more than he could afford, I remember* . . . The gift in question was a fan of delicately worked cream brocade and lace mounted on ivory sticks.

"Oh, what a lovely thought!" Kate exclaimed, wafting it gently to cool her face. "I remember seeing it once when I was quite small. I thought it the most delicate and beautiful thing in all the world!"

"Your mama was a great beauty in her day," the marchioness reminisced with a sigh. "We could none of us hold a candle to her. She might have looked as high as she pleased, but she had eyes for no one but your father."

"She never speaks much of that time, or of my grandparents. I know they did not approve of the marriage . . ." The note of censure in her voice did not escape her godmother.

"Lord and Lady Welby had great hopes for Elizabeth, you see," she said. "Your father was, at that time, a struggling young doctor with little to recommend him, and she was younger than you are now, with very little experience of life."

"But they loved one another! Surely that is the most important thing of all?"

Lady St. Clair heard the passion in the young girl's voice, and was carried back, so far back it seemed, now. "Oh, I was never in doubt about that, my dear. At eighteen, it was the very stuff of romance to me, and I did everything I could to aid and abet them without a thought for the pain it would cause." She sighed. "We were so young, so full of the certainty that we were right."

"And you were!"

"Indeed, yes. I have never doubted that. But with the wisdom of years, I can also appreciate the bitter disappointment and heartbreak that Elizabeth's elopement caused the Welbys. She was their only child, born when they had almost given up hope . . . and she had grown to be a beauty, with the world at her feet. Elizabeth could have had the pick of the Marriage Mart—"

"The Marriage Mart!"

"You may scoff, my dear, but it meant a great deal to them to see their only daughter well be-stowed—a wish all parents cherish for their daugh-ters, your own parents included. Instead, she chose to elope with a near-penniless nobody—for so your father seemed to be in their eyes," she added hastily, seeing how dangerously her godchild's eyes sparkled.

"Even so, to withhold even the slightest contact for all those years." Kate's voice was hard. "I can-not forgive them, for I know how it has grieved Mama."

"I suspect that is also the cruellest misery for the Welbys—never to have seen their grandchildren. Your grandparents are old now . . . they haven't been to Town for many years, and I daresay they have learned to live with the bitter fruits of their stubbornness, but even so . . ." The marchioness saw that Kate was not convinced, and thought it best to refrain from upsetting her further on this, of all days. "Ah, well, what is done, is done."

She stood up. "And now, my dear, I must go and rest for an hour or so if I am to be fresh for what is like to be a very long evening. I would advise you to do likewise," her eyes twinkled, "except that if I

were young again, I would scoff at such advice. Do
not forget that the *frisseur* is coming to arrange
your hair at five o'clock. The ball does not begin
until nine o'clock, but we shall be receiving the dinner guests at six and sit down to dine at seven."

Left alone, Kate felt too restless to settle to anything. She re-read Kit's letter, seeing him in her
mind's eye, so full of energy and *joie de vivre*, and as
she fingered the little fan a great wave of homesickness threatened to overwhelm her. What was she
doing here in this great house where the ghost of
another still held sway, when almost everyone she
cared about was miles away? If it weren't for Lady
St. Clair, she would not care a fig for tonight.

And then she glanced at the little pile of gifts and
good wishes, and in spite of herself, the little bub-
bles of excitement erupted again and would not be
contained. How on earth was she to pass the next
few hours? Finally, she gathered all her gifts together, resolved to go to her room and try to rest.

But on the way she passed a room that Blaise had
referred to briefly as the Rose Saloon, which, Kate
remembered, had included among the pretty
gilded furnishings that gave the room its name, a
spinet. Music, she decided, would be just the thing
to calm her agitation. She had never played a
spinet, but it could not be so very different from
any other keyboard instrument.

The marquess was on his way downstairs when
he heard the distant sound—someone was playing
the spinet. For a moment he paused, shaken to the
core, wondering if his recent excesses had induced
his mind to play tricks. But the music, marred by
the occasional wrong note, was surely no figment
of a disordered mind.

Kate, absorbed in mastering an instrument which
was unfamiliar to her, was not immediately aware

of the door opening. Even so, something impelled her to look up. The marquess was standing in the open doorway, one white-knuckled hand grasping the handle as if to support himself. Gone was the disheveled look of the early morning, but the elegance of his blue-tailed coat, pristine cravat, and buff pantaloons merely served to accentuate his pallor, and the pain in his eyes was almost palpable.

Kate scrambled inelegantly to her feet. "Forgive me, I had not meant to . . . that is, I suddenly craved a little music, and . . ."

"For God's sake, don't apologize," he said jerkily. "Musical instruments are meant to be played, are they not? And this particular one has been silent too long."

Immediately she understood. "It belonged to your wife. I should have realized. I'm so s—"

"Don't!" he said again. He walked forward until he was very close. "What were you playing?"

"Part of the rondo from a Mozart sonata—rather badly, I'm afraid. I am more used to a pianoforte."

"It is all one to me. I am a philistine when it comes to the finer points of music and musical instruments." His long, slim fingers caressed the satin wood almost sensuously. "But Lucinda loved this spinet, for all that it is quite old. It has been here for as long as I can remember."

Kate, mesmerized by the movement of his fingers, pulled herself together with an effort and endeavored to turn his thoughts away from Lucinda by gathering up her presents and *billet doux*, saying with a laugh, "Am I not fortunate? So many kind people. Mama has sent me a very special gift . . ." She spread out the fan and related its history. "A letter from Kit, too!"

The marquess, watching her animated face, could detect in those sparkling green eyes no lingering disgust of him following their early morning encounter. Nor was there any sign of the pity, which would have been more humiliating.

Nothing, however could have equaled his own disgust upon gaining the privacy of his room early that morning. Hobb, his valet, had, as ever, allowed no hint of reproach to make itself known. But the looking glass placed in his own line of vision had presented him with an image which, illuminated by sunlight, had suddenly filled him with revulsion, so that he groaned aloud.

"I have taken the liberty of preparing one of my potions, my lord," murmured his discreet, impeccably mannered valet, who had been with him for as long as he could remember.

"The devil you have." Blaise swung around unsteadily, and groaned, his head in his hands. "Do I not disgust you, Hobb?"

"Indeed no, my lord. I would not presume to pass judgment." Hobb had hesitated. "We have been through much together, my lord, and I hope I understand your lordship well enough to make allowances."

"You're a good fellow, Hobb. Better than I deserve. But I disgust myself. I had fully resolved to end this wallowing in what's past and gone." His laugh ended in a groan. "And this time I mean to do it. It don't sit well with me, and besides *she* wouldn't have liked it."

"No, my lord. If you say so."

"I do say so, Hobb. Beginning tonight. Miss Sheridan's debut—mustn't let Mama down. So, bring forth your noxious potion, then you may lead me to that bath."

"Very good, my lord."

It would be overoptimistic to say that today a watershed had been reached and passed, but a new beginning had been made, and this time, by God, he would not fail. . . .

He saw that Kate was still watching him, a faintly puzzled look in her eyes. He cleared his throat.

"Forgive me. A letter from your brother, you said. Is he quite well?"

Kate laughed. "Oh, very well—and in prodigiously good spirits. His talk is all of balls and what fine sport is to be had—but that is Kit all over." She sobered suddenly. "Even so, the battle must come, must it not?"

It was not really a question, and he knew she would not be fobbed off with anything less than the truth. "I'm afraid so. Bonaparte has to be stopped for good this time. And soon. But Wellington will win. I haven't a doubt of it."

"Nor have I. And Kit will be fine. It's just . . . I wish he were here."

The yearning in her voice was more obvious than she realized. He said with unexpected gentleness, "You are very fond of him?"

"It is impossible to be otherwise, for all that he can be so insufferably single-minded." She said it so defiantly that he smiled. It changed his whole face, making him seem suddenly younger and . . . She pulled her thoughts up before they strayed into unfamiliar territory. "However, I should be well used to his long absences by now."

"You will have to make do with me, instead," he said.

"You?"

"In the absence of any immediate family, I believe it falls to me to lead you out tonight."

"Oh, I had not expected . . ." she began hurriedly, "I hope your mother did not . . ." What a mull she was making of it. "That is, you must not feel obliged to do so. You have been more than kind already."

He lifted a quizzical eyebrow, and again she was afforded a glimpse of that young man his mother had talked about so wistfully. Kate had no idea what had induced such a marked change, but it was certainly a change for the better, and she could only welcome it.

"You blush quite delightfully, Kate. But I will not tease you further. It will give me great pleasure if you will do me the honor of allowing me to lead you out in the opening dance."

"Well, if you are sure," she said, determined to be totally honest with him. "The thing is, although I have been to several balls in Dublin with my parents, I doubt I am more than reasonably competent . . ."

"Is that all?" He took her hand, and his smile became a deep-throated chuckle which melted all resistance. "I, on the other hand, am considered to be more than competent, so you may safely entrust yourself to me."

# *Eleven*

It was an evening Kate would never forget.

"Oh, miss, you do look lovely! There won't be
nobody finer . . . an' that hairdresser's done your
hair a treat . . . an' them flowers from 'is lordship, a
perfick match, they are! There won't be no one to
touch you!"

Kate smiled a little at this sweeping judgment,
but, if nothing else, it gave her confidence. For suddenly all her protestations about the absurdity of
making her formal curtsy to society seemed to
count for nothing as she took her place beside
Blaise and the marchioness in the gallery leading to
the blue drawing room to receive the dinner guests,
clutching the fresh pink roses in a small gilt holder
which matched perfectly the silk ones on her
gown—a totally unexpected gift from the marquess
which had been delivered to her room earlier.

"I can't think how you knew," she had said,
blushing a little as she thanked him.

"It is but a trifle," he replied abruptly. "The roses
came from the hothouses at Kimberley. A small me-
mento, if you care to think of it in that way."

"I shall certainly treasure it as such. I am
ashamed to admit that after all my much vaunted
determination to remain quite calm, I am as full of
nerves as any impressionable green girl. Is that not
absurd?"

"My dear, you have nothing to fear. I have never seen you look more lovely," murmured the marchioness, who herself seemed a little less at ease than usual.

"Nor I, you, dear ma'am," Kate said, and meant it, for her godmother, in a gown of lavender silk, which echoed her sparkling eyes, looked too ridiculously young and pretty to be a dowager with a full-grown son. A dainty lace cap encrusted with amethysts nestled in the fairness of her hair, echoing the deep purple amethysts that circled her neck.

"Oh, what nonsense!" her ladyship protested. "I am past all that sort of thing. This is your night, and everyone will be too busy looking at you to notice me. You will turn all heads. Will she not, Blaise?" she demanded of her son.

His long, considering look brought the faint color up under Kate's skin. The marchioness may have exaggerated, but she would have been a great goose not to have realized how well she looked. But as to whether her looks would meet with his lordship's approval? That was another matter. He was silent for so long that she grew nervous, and as always when she was nervous, her tongue ran away with her.

"I'm afraid I came close to breaking the hairdresser's heart. Poor Monsieur Pierre—such a verbose little man. He was quite desperate to persuade me to have my hair cut very short, in a style he called *á la Tite*. Apparently it is all the rage. But I couldn't bring myself to agree . . ."

"I should think not, indeed," cried the marchioness. "You have such beautiful hair, it would be criminal to cut it."

Blaise too was surprised by the indignation that shook him at the mere possibility. In the event, the disappointed *frisseur* had excelled himself by creating an intricate Grecian knot that shone like burnished copper in the lamplight, into which he had woven a rope of tiny seed pearls. A few tendrils of hair had been coaxed to fall in loose curls about her ears. Thus exposed, the purity of Kate's cheek and jawline acquired a vulnerable quality which moved Blaise more than he cared to admit.

"You need have no fear—you look quite lovely," he said at last, and there was something in the way he said it that made his mother look swiftly at him.

As the dinner guests continued to arrive, Kate grew in confidence, greeting each one with a pleasant smile and responding to their good wishes with an appropriate word. They seemed, she confided to her godmother, to include a great many members of the nobility and at least one renowned member of the diplomatic set, who, murmured Blaise irreverently, cherished a long-time tendresse for his mama—a charge which she refuted even as a blush betrayed her, making her look younger than ever and filling Kate with curiosity. Also among their number were some of the most illustrious doyens of society, some she already knew, such as Lady Cowper and Lady Sefton, whom she liked very much, and Lady Jersey, and many others whom she had not previously met. In spite of her resolve not to succumb to nerves, it was something of a relief to see Sir Charles and Lady Melchester with Chloe and Charlie Stanford.

"How pretty you look tonight, Chloe," she exclaimed, admiring her gown of spider gauze. "That is exactly the right shade of blue to match your eyes."

"Oh, I'm well enough, but not half so fine as you," Chloe agreed cheerfully, without a trace of envy.

"I should say not," Charlie exclaimed. "Not by a long way. May I be allowed to say how jolly splendid you look, Kate. Always do, of course," he added hurriedly, lest she should misinterpret his compliment. "Still—never seen you looking finer. There won't be anyone to hold a candle to you this evening. I suppose it would be too much to hope that you would honor me with the first dance . . ."

Kate caught Mr. Merivale's eye and as one eyebrow lifted imperceptibly, she had the greatest difficulty keeping a straight face as she told Charlie regretfully that the marquess was before him.

"Yes, of course . . . should have realized. Protocol and all that . . . but later, perhaps . . ."

Kate said she would be delighted to dance with him later.

"You spoke with such conviction that for a moment I almost believed you—as he did. Poor boy—never thinks before he speaks." Mr. Merivale put up his glass when everyone seemed to have arrived and they were alone for a moment. "Though in complimenting you so lavishly he speaks no less than the truth. I detect the unmistakable genius of La Fanchon," he added with unerring percipience. "You do her credit."

Kate's eyes twinkled. "Why, thank you, Mr. Merivale. I shall take that as a true compliment, coming as it does from so discerning a man of fashion."

"Kate, you disappoint me," chided his lordship, arriving in time to hear her. "I thought you had better taste than to account this fribble a doyen of fashion."

She looked from one to the other, not knowing quite how to reply. Mr. Merivale was, as always, impeccably turned out in black breeches and a close-fitting wine-colored coat, the collar points of his shirt so high that he could not turn his head, his cravat a miracle of complexity. Yet, privately, she was obliged to admit that she preferred the starker elegance of the marquess's black and white, with slim black trousers and a coat cut by a master, his white cravat complex but restrained, an embroidered brocade waistcoat the only touch of extravagance.

"To be honest, gentlemen, I have always found comparisons to be odious," she finally confessed, her eyes still brimming with mirth. "Also, I learned a long time ago not to come between a man and his wardrobe . . ."

"Coward," said the marquess softly.

"Not at all. Sure, it can't be entirely coincidence that when the Lord created us, it was to the male peacock he gave that preposterous tail!"

There was a moment of silence, then he laughed aloud, a spontaneous sound that reached his mother, making her turn in surprise, which quickly became pleasure as she saw whence it came.

"She's outflanked the two of us, Gervase," Blaise admitted. "Rolled us up, horse, foot, and guns!"

"I shall survive," drawled Mr. Merivale, taking the verdict in good part.

The marchioness, watching them, allowed herself a moment of indulgence—to hope.

"So that is your young protégée, Alicia," murmured a familiar voice. "A charming creature. You are to be complimented, my dear."

"Dominic!" She turned, looking up—a long way up, it seemed, for she had forgotten how tall he was—and her cheeks warmed a little as Sir Dominic Lazenby, plenipotentiary par excellence to his majesty's government, took her outstretched hand and raised it gallantly to his lips, which lingered just long enough to raise a blush. He had grown a little heavier with the years, but he was still a handsome man, splendidly attired, his dark mane of hair still apparently without a trace of gray, aided no doubt by a liberal application of macassar oil.

"Blaise told me you were back in London, so I sent an invitation on the off-chance that you might spare us a few hours from your busy life."

"How could I deny myself the opportunity of seeing you, my dear." He smiled down at her, showing no inclination to release her hand. "The only woman I have ever loved."

"Dominic!" She felt her cheeks grow warm as she tugged her hand free, and saw his smile deepen. "You must not say such things, even in jest! Goodness, it is an age since last we met."

"Too long by far," he agreed, amused by her embarrassment. "During which time, I vow, you have grown younger and prettier."

"Hush," she pleaded, half laughing. "You will put me to the blush."

"Why not, when you blush so delightfully? And how is that son of yours? Bad business, that. Can't remember who told me. And that pretty wife of his, far too young to die."

"Yes, indeed. Blaise took it very badly. But I have great hopes that he is at last recovering."

"Good. Good. Don't do to dwell on such matters." His eyes twinkled. "Still, no need to ask how you do, m'dear."

"Nor I, you," she returned swiftly, before he had time to embarrass her again. "Traveling obviously agrees with you."

"Breath of life," he agreed. "I was the best part of two years in Brazil, and on my return was sent almost immediately to France, then Vienna. Negotiations were rudely interrupted by Bonaparte's antics, but there was still much to be discussed. And finally I was summoned to London."

"Well, I am delighted that you were." The marchioness became aware that Jameson was endeavoring to catch her eye. "Dominic, forgive me, but there is a very important matter I must attend to. I am sure you know almost everyone here, so I feel no compunction in leaving you for a short while. There will be all the time in the world to talk later."

He smiled wryly and raised her hand once more to his lips. "I shall hold you to that, m'dear."

The marquess, who had already been primed by Jameson, crossed the room to rescue Kate from the clutches of a tedious bore, with murmurs of an urgent summons elsewhere, and steered her through the by-now crowded room toward the far door.

"Blaise, I protest," she exclaimed, bemused and amused at one and the same time as she made a half-hearted attempt to hold back, and found her arm firmly held as he propelled her onward. "Poor Mrs. Arbuthnot—she patently disbelieved your tale of summonses, and will by now be thinking us both quite mad."

"Let her," he said ruthlessly as heads turned to watch them pass. "The lady's opinion is of little interest to me."

"How shocking!" She had never seen him in this mood before. "Blaise! I really must protest, everyone is looking at us. Where are you taking me?"

"You will soon find out."

They had by now reached the door of a small anteroom leading off the gallery, where Jameson waited to open the door for her. Kate paused to look inquiringly at Blaise, and saw that he was almost smiling.

Jameson cleared his throat. "If you would care to step inside, Miss Sheridan."

"Oh, really, this is absurd! Why is everyone being so mysterious . . ." Kate began, and then on the threshold froze, her breath caught, her eyes widening in mingled joy and disbelief, scarcely aware of the marchioness, seeing only Mama, smiling, wear-

ing her best silver-gray gown, and her father, looking very distinguished in dark coat and breeches,
his prematurely white hair at odds with his lively,
humorous face.

"I don't believe it!" she gasped. "Mama . . . ?
Pa . . . ? Oh, this is the most wonderful . . ." She
caught up her skirts and ran forward, her arms
thrown out to hug each of them in turn.

Blaise, who had followed her in almost unnoticed, watched the exuberant, unfeigned joy of their
reunion with something akin to jealousy as memories, deliberately blotted out, stirred in his subcon-
scious—of Lucinda running into his arms with the
same exuberance, and a time when every day was
filled with joy.

"Careful, my darling," Lady Elizabeth was be-
seeching her daughter huskily, halfway between
laughter and tears. "You will spoil your lovely
dress."

"Oh heavens! But I don't understand . . . how are
you here? I never expected . . . it was only this
morning that I received your letter, and the little
fan . . ." She held out her arm. "See?"

"We couldn't be entirely sure of getting away,
m'dear, on account of your Aunt Kitty," her father
explained in his whimsical Irish way. "She had
promised to come and stay, but you know Kitty's
promises—they have a way of crumbling like one
of Nan's famous piecrusts . . ."

"And we dared not raise your hopes for fear of
disappointing you," her mother continued. "But
this darling godmother of yours, or rather, it was
Blaise, I believe . . ." she smiled at him as he inclined his head, "obliged us by engaging a suite at
the Pulteney Hotel, just to be on the safe side, so as
not to spoil the surprise."

"So everyone knew except me!" Kate tried to
sound reproachful, but the happiness kept bub-

bling up. "Ah, well, I forgive you all, for this wonderful surprise has made my day quite perfect."

"Quite perfect," echoed Miss Priddy, fluttering in
the background like a small brown lace moth and
dabbing at her eyes. The marchioness had deliberately kept her busy in the background for fear she
would ruin everything in her excitement. "So affecting . . ."

"I still can't believe it. How long are you here for,
Mama?"

"A whole month, or so we hope. Your father has
several friends he wishes to look up, so we shall
have all the time in the world to talk."

The marquess became aware that Jameson was
hovering at the door and drew his mother's attention to the fact.

"Now, do come along everyone," she said. "Dinner awaits us. And I have put you all together, so
you may talk as much as you like."

Kate had no memory of what she ate, or to whom
she spoke other than her parents during dinner and
as the guests arrived for the ball. The evening had
already by far exceeded all her expectations, and
anything else could only be a benefaction.

The ballroom was everything a ballroom should
be—all white and silver, and fragrant with the
scent of the flowers arranged in great swathes of
color at either end of the room. On a dais at the far
end, the orchestra was tuning up, and the whole
scene was softened by the glow from several large
chandeliers, which, though Kate was unaware of it,
cast the same soft glow across the face she lifted to
Blaise as he came toward her, no doubt to lead her
out for the opening country dance.

He looked pale, his face carved in a travesty of a
polite smile. It must be sheer torture for him, she
thought, for he will have performed the same ritual
with Lucinda many times in this very room. Her

throat ached with pity for him, yet he must not know it.

"I am of course deeply honored to have you lead me out, Blaise," she said, looking up at him in mock reproof. "Though I am not sure I have yet forgiven you for deceiving me so convincingly. There you were, this afternoon, allowing me to chatter on about my parents and the history of this fan, and all without so much as a hint . . ."

She saw him almost physically drag himself back from the pain of memory to say with a forced smile, "But the secret was not mine to bestow. You would not have me betray a confidence?"

"Perhaps not, but when one considers the deviousness of it all . . . to betray not even the tiniest hint! Oh, well . . ." She laughed, unable to keep up the pretense any longer.

"As to leading you out, it seemed the perfect way to allay any hint of suspicion. But now that your father is safely arrived, I must, of necessity, surrender the privilege to him."

"Of course," Kate agreed brightly. He would no doubt be delighted to be spared, she thought, and wondered why the notion should depress her so. "It was a generous thought."

"It was Mama's thought, actually. And very right and proper. Perhaps I may be fortunate later—if your card is not totally filled?"

"You need not feel the least obligation . . ."

Blaise held out a hand for the card, and after a moment she surrendered it.

"You are popular, I see. And quite right too. Ah, I see there is a waltz free after supper."

He was so insistent, his eyes so brilliant, that for a brief moment she wondered if he might be drunk.

"I'm not very proficient at waltzing . . ."

"But I am, so you need have no fear . . ." He scrawled his name, and handed the card back to her. "Ah, here is your father come to claim you." He took her hand and led her forward. "Dr. Sheridan, I leave you to do the honors."

"Thank you, m'lord. Very generous of you to surrender your place to me."

"My pleasure, sir. Kate—until later." He bowed and left them.

"An interesting young man," mused her father under cover of the applause as he led Kate out. "Tragedy does strange things to people."

"He is still deeply unhappy," she murmured, and then determinedly put Blaise from her mind and gave herself up to the sheer pleasure of dancing with her father, who was as elegant a performer as many a man half his age.

"Darling Pa, I can't tell you what it means to me to have you and Mama here," she said as they went down the line. "I can't think how you managed it, for I know how much you dislike delegating your work to others."

"All things are relative, my dear girl. It distressed me far more to see your mama trying desperately to hide her longing to be here. Not a word was said, mind," he smiled, "but we have been together too long for me to remain unaware of her misery. When I tackled her, she said she was thinking of Kit, and that was a part of it, for sure. But I knew fine where she longed to be."

As the dance came to an end, she said abruptly, "Kit will be all right, won't he, Pa?"

"The thing you have to remember, Kate, is that Kit has ever had a will of his own and he is doing the thing he loves most. The rest is in God's hands."

"You are right, of course."

From that moment on, Kate hardly had time to draw breath. She was partnered in an elegant quadrille by Mr. Merivale, and had her toes stepped on by Charlie Stanford in the country dance.

"Sorry. Deuced clumsy of me," he stammered, red-faced and looking very uncomfortable as he pulled at his cravat, which was clearly much too high and tight for comfort. "Not at my best in a ballroom, d'ye see . . ."

"You needn't apologize, Charlie," she said kindly. "It would be a boring world if we were to excel at everything."

"My point entirely! Outdoor pursuits more to my taste, d'ye see. Give me a horse or a gun and I'm much more at ease."

Kate remembered Blaise's opinion of Charlie's horsemanship, and was hard put to it not to smile. She said diplomatically, "Well, there you are, then. That proves my point."

The dance seemed to go on forever. And even when it finally did come to an end, she had the greatest difficulty in shaking him off without giving offense. It was Sir Dominic in the end who came to her rescue.

"Miss Sheridan," he exclaimed, approaching with a genial smile. "I have been searching for you everywhere. Lady St. Clair charged me most straightly to find you and bring you to her."

Charlie, overawed by the presence of so important a gentleman, bowed extravagantly and excused himself.

"Thank you, sir."

Sir Dominic's eyes twinkled. "For what? For seeing off an egregious bore so that I may have a pretty young lady to myself for a few moments?"

Kate, unsure how to deal with so accomplished a flirt, scarcely knew how to answer. "Charlie isn't really so bad. He is very good-natured . . ." She saw the glint in his eyes. "It's just that he can't seem to take a hint." She hesitated before asking diffidently, "Did my godmother really send you?"

He laughed so heartily that several people

looked their way. "Perhaps not, but she would undoubtedly have done so had she known the circumstances." He offered his arm. "And you would not deny a harmless old *roué* the pleasure of escorting you in to supper?"

Kate felt laughter bubbling up in return as she laid her fingertips on the black velvet sleeve. "Are you really a *roué*, sir? What fun. Only think what consequence it will give me to be seen with you."

The marquess, watching from across the room, felt a twinge of annoyance—and, could it be, jealousy?

A string quartet had been engaged to play throughout supper, which was held in a large salon adjoining the ballroom. Here, every kind of delicacy was to be found, from salmon to syllabub, from *mousseline* of trout and goose patties to exotic fruits brought up from the hothouses at Kimberley. And as a centerpiece, the chef's creation par excellence, a huge swan of snowy-white meringue, encircled by tiny swans floating on a lake of *crème Chantilly*.

Kate, filled with nervous anticipation at the prospect of waltzing with Blaise, ate very little, but drank two glasses of champagne to bolster her courage. He, for all his earlier protestations that it was not his role, seemed to be playing the host to perfection.

But supper was over all too soon, and the moment had arrived. She told herself it was the champagne that made her a trifle light-headed as Blaise whirled her around the room, his hand intimately warm through the thin silk of her gown, drawing her ever closer, his tautly muscled thigh occasionally touching hers as they dipped and swayed; it must be the champagne, too, that caused the oddest sensations to course through her in response to his touch. A part of her longed for it to be over, while another traitorous part wanted it never to end.

But end it did. He had not spoken once throughout, and as he led her off the floor, he thanked her almost curtly. His eyes, overbright, seeming to be looking through rather than at her, so that she wondered for a moment whether he had been drinking except that he could not have danced so well had he been anything but sober. Perhaps he had been fantasizing, imagining that she was Lucinda. It was a possibility that she found unaccountably depressing.

It was some time later that Lady St. Clair beckoned Kate over and asked her to find Blaise. "Lady Jersey talks of leaving shortly. I did not see him among the dancers during the quadrille, and he really should be here to say his adieus."

It was only then that Kate realized she hadn't seen him since their waltz. "I'll ask Jameson. He will know."

But Jameson was of little help, except to say that had not seen his lordship leave the ballroom. "I will send Henry to look for him."

Kate could have left the matter there, but if Blaise was badly foxed, she did not want him found by one of the servants. Perhaps he just needed a few moments of quiet. But with so many rooms to choose from, where would he go?

And then she thought of the Rose Saloon.

# Twelve

He was standing in a shaft of moonlight, bowed over the little spinet, his hands splayed out across the lid, with every inch of him sending out vibrations of indecision, verging on despair.

The Rose Saloon was not among those open to the guests. Kate had opened the door so quietly that he seemed not to have heard her, and now that she was here, she was not sure what to do for the best. Perhaps she ought simply to go back and tell the marchioness that he was indisposed.

While she still hesitated, he said abruptly, without looking up, "Go away, and shut that damned door behind you."

"That is not a very polite way to address your honored guest," she said with surprising calmness.

"You," he ground out, with a travesty of a laugh. "I might have known you would not leave well alone." But he made no attempt to move or look up. "How did you know where to find me?"

"I didn't. It was pure chance."

Kate closed the door, lest any of the servants should overhear. There was still light enough from the windows to enable her to see him clearly. "Blaise, you are neglecting your duties, and your mother has need of you."

It was a presumptuous thing to say and she had no idea how it would be received. When he did not immediately reply, she gathered up her courage and, with heart beating uncomfortably fast, she walked across the room to stand beside him. "Blaise, I know this must have been a difficult evening for you, but—"

"Oh, so you know, do you?" He lifted his head suddenly to face her. "And do you know why it has been so damnably difficult?" His eyes glittered blackly in the moonlight. "Do you?" He seized her arms, his fingers digging painfully into her flesh.

"I can hazard a guess." The words were thick in her throat.

"You are good at guessing—as when you found me. But this time you would be only partly right, dear innocent Kate, in your pretty green gown." He pulled her forward, one arm enclosing her in a band of steel, the other lifting her face to his, his mouth closing on hers, fiercely at first, robbing her of breath, then probing until her lips parted, and she was filled with a trembling ecstasy, her whole body on fire, melting with sensations she had not known she was capable of until now.

When at last he released her, she felt bereft and lightheaded at one and the same time, and was obliged to grasp his coat for fear of falling. At once his arms came around her.

"Forgive me. I had not meant that to happen," he said unsteadily. "Though, God forgive me, I have been fighting a strong desire to kiss you all evening."

Surprise was piling upon surprise, and she was in no state to make sense of it at present. She struggled to reassert a sense of reality. "Blaise, you mustn't . . . you don't know what you are saying . . ."

"Oh, but I do! Perhaps you don't realize how tantalizing you appear—how refreshing is that curious mixture of innocence and commonsense . . ."

"Please, you mustn't say such things! Not now. I

have to . . . we have to . . . your mother . . ." she began tremulously. "Oh, lordy, how am I to face your mother and everyone . . ."

"Don't try. Stay here with me," he said urgently. "I've been such a fool, Kate . . . we have to talk . . ."

"I cannot." Her mouth felt bruised and trembling, but with an effort, she fought for some semblance of calm. "You know I can't, not now, and neither can you. Lady Jersey is about to leave and you cannot shame your mother by abandoning your duty."

For a moment his brows descended in an ominous frown, and then he shrugged his shoulders. "You and your sense of duty. But you are right, of course—as usual. Come along." He stretched out a hand.

In the corridor, which was mercifully deserted, she said, "Do I look—?"

"Thoroughly kissed?"

"Hush!"

He eyed her quizzically, and her mouth quivered beneath his inspection. "I daresay no one will suspect."

"I don't see how they can fail to! You will have to go on ahead. If we arrive together, my blushes will betray me, and then everyone will know."

In the ballroom, a quadrille was coming to an end, and Lady St. Clair was frantically wondering how she was to account for the absence of the two people she most needed at this moment. In particular, Kate's future could stand or fall at the whim of Lady Jersey. She was in general exceedingly amiable, but it would not do for her to feel she was being slighted. And she was presently gathering up her fan and her gloves.

"Blaise is not here—or Kate," whispered the marchioness, her eyes lifting in mute appeal to Sir

Dominic. His eyebrows were wildly quizzical, but he came at once to her aid.

"Why, never tell me you are leaving us, ma'am," he exclaimed, stepping forward and exerting every ounce of his considerable charm on Lady Jersey. "Why, I have scarcely had the pleasure of your company for more than a moment, and I did so wish to seek your opinion on a most delicate matter concerning . . ."

Lady Jersey sat back again, flattered, and graciously begged him to be seated, which he did with an expert flick of his coattails, lowering his voice discreetly as he launched into a scurrilous and utterly convincing rumor concerning a joint acquaintance whom neither of them cared for. Since scandal was the breath of life to her ladyship, she would not now think of leaving until every scrap of information had been garnered.

Nevertheless, it was with a profound sense of relief that Lady St. Clair saw her son approaching.

"Blaise! At last! I had begun to wonder . . . Have you seen Kate? She went to ask Jameson to look for you."

"Which she did, Mama. And behold, I am here."

His calmness was doubly provoking. "Yes, that is very well, but now Kate is gone missing, which is quite as bad. Oh, what a coil! Lady Jersey was on the point of leaving some five minutes since. I have had to call upon Dominic's most persuasive powers to hold her thus far . . ."

"Kate will be here at any moment, I am sure," he said soothingly.

"Well, I hope you may be right. But poor Mr. Wycherly was most put out because she missed the contredanse she had promised to him."

Blaise put up his glass to survey the rotund dandy, his face red with pique. "It takes very little to ruffle Wycherly's feathers, but you may be sure

Kate will know exactly how to smooth him down when she arrives."

"That is all very well for you to say . . ." The marchioness found his levity less than helpful, and in other circumstances might have wondered at it. But just now . . .

"And indeed, here she comes."

Her ladyship followed his direction and was relieved to see Kate approaching. Her goddaughter's color was a trifle high, and it was to be hoped that she was not unwell.

"No, indeed, dear ma'am," Kate assured her when questioned, avoiding meeting Blaise's eyes. "I am quite well—merely a trifle warm. But I had not meant to be away so long. Poor Mr. Wycherly. I must apologize to him at once."

"Not quite at once, my dear."

A light laugh tinged with amusement drew her attention to Lady Jersey, who was rapping Dominic playfully across the knuckles. "You are a wicked rogue," they heard her say to him as she gathered up her belongings once more. "One is never sure when to believe you."

"Word of a gentleman, ma'am, I promise you— word of a gentleman," Dominic vowed with a chuckle, glancing quickly across to see that all was satisfactorily resolved. "When all is made public, you will see that I am right. Must you leave?" He was all attention. "Then pray allow me to assist you."

Lady Jersey was in excellent spirits as she left. "You have done well, child," she told Kate benevolently as she left. "I have no doubt you will take." And to Lady St. Clair, "A pity there is no fortune, but a most agreeable evening, Alicia. You will naturally be requiring vouchers for Almack's. I will see that you receive them," she said as she sailed out with both Blaise and Sir Dominic to see her safely to her carriage.

"Well, thank goodness for that," sighed her ladyship, sinking back into the sofa as the two men returned. "How tactless she can be! But never mind. Dominic, you were quite wonderful!"

"I was, wasn't I? Wouldn't have done it for anyone but you, m'dear." He sat down beside her, a wicked glint in his eyes. "Which reminds me, I shall expect to be properly recompensed in due course."

"Dominic!" She affected to be shocked. "I cannot think what you mean."

"Then why are you blushing so delightfully?"

"I am sure it is nothing more than the heat of the room."

"If you say so, my dear." His hand sought hers under the folds of her gown, and abandoning raillery, he said softly, "You know, of course, that I have been in love with you since your own come-out, though you only ever had eyes for Edward. And as he was my best friend, what could I do?"

"Dominic!" Lady St. Clair felt a sudden wild leaping of the blood, and glanced hurriedly around, but with a waltz in full swing, there was no one in earshot but Miss Priddy, and she was in a world of her own, her fan moving to the music, a faraway look in her eyes. "You really must not . . ."

"Must not what?"

"Speak of such things . . . hold my hand . . ." But she made no attempt to move it.

"Why not?"

"Because . . . because it was all so long ago, and we are past all that sort of thing, and anyway, someone might hear." She sighed deeply, seduced by memory. "Oh, but what days they were, to be sure!"

"And could be again. Did I tell you I am to be based here in London for the foreseeable future?"

"You are?" Again, she felt it—that wild surge. I am too old for all this, she thought, but the feeling would not be denied. "That is splendid news." And then hurriedly, lest her voice should betray her, "Ah, see, the dance is ending," she said, and wondered why he laughed as he released her hand.

In an attempt to change the subject, she said, "Blaise is in a very odd mood, all of a sudden. If I did not know better, I would suspect him of being foxed . . . not that he would be so foolish on such an occasion."

Sir Dominic followed her gaze, and was in time to see Blaise throw back his head and laugh at some comment made by Lady Melchester. He also saw Kate turn upon hearing that laugh, and was experienced enough to recognize the raw emotion that flared momentarily in the young girl's eyes. Well, here's a pretty turn of events, he thought. Please God, he won't break the child's heart.

"Have no fear. He's just being a good host, m'dear," he said reassuringly.

On the far side of the ballroom, Mr. Merivale also stood watching Blaise watching Kate laughing and talking animatedly to Mr. Wycherly, as the sets began to form for a country dance.

"Looks particularly fine this evening, don't she?" he observed.

"Who?"

"Young Kate, who else. A veritable Juno. A kind of innocent radiance about her, wouldn't you say?"

Blaise dragged his gaze away almost guiltily. "I suppose so. But then she has every reason . . . it has been a special evening, and crowned with the added excitement of her parents' arrival."

"Oh, quite . . . Still, never seen her look quite like

that," Mr. Merivale mused. "Be a tragedy if anyone were to prick the bubble, trifle with her affections . . ."

There was a long silence between them, broken only by the swell of conversation around them and the tuning up of the orchestra.

"Only an unspeakable cad would do such a thing," Blaise agreed slowly.

"Quite," said Mr. Merivale.

Blaise slept fitfully that night, slipping in and out of a confused dream in which he was surrounded by crowds of beautiful young women, searching desperately for one who remained just out of reach, and from which he awoke drowned in perspiration.

The ball was acknowledged by the *ton* to have been a resounding success and heralded the beginning of a period when the knocker in Mount Street was never still, and invitations daily littered her ladyship's mantelshelf.

"At this rate, my love, we shall not be a single night at home."

"You are really loving all this, aren't you?" Kate said, seeing the sparkle in her godmother's eyes.

"I would not say 'love,' exactly, but it is very agreeable to be among one's friends. And I am so enjoying having the pleasure of your mama's company after all these years. Letters are very well, but it is not the same. And it will do her a world of good to renew her acquaintance with old friends." Lady St. Clair eyed her young goddaughter shrewdly. "And do not tell me that you are not equally happy, for I shall not believe you."

"That would be very perverse of me," Kate freely acknowledged. "And it would be untrue, for I am having a splendid time, and it is wonderful to have

Mama and Papa here to enjoy it with me, even if the hours are flying much too fast."

She did not mention Blaise; indeed, she could not have done so without betraying her feelings, ashamed as she was of the curious melting in her limbs that assailed her whenever she recalled that heart-stopping moment in the Rose Saloon.

In any case, she had swiftly come to the conclusion that, whatever he may have inferred in that moment of weakness, he had as soon forgotten in the cold clear light of day—and she must do likewise, and put aside any lingering foolishness. If he was pleasant with her, she would respond accordingly, treating him much as she would Kit, were he here.

# Thirteen

Kate's parents had moved from the Pulteney to Mount Street for the remainder of their stay. Her father spent much of his time looking up former cronies, eager to learn of any recent advances in medicine, new remedies for old ills, secure in the knowledge that his wife would be able to fill her hours equally contentedly in similar fashion.

Only one matter clouded Lady Elizabeth's pleasure, apart from the ever-present worry of her eldest son, who could soon find himself at war again, and that was the rift with her parents. In the early days of her marriage she had written to them regularly, telling them as each child came along, even about the two early ones that had been stillborn. But, to her continuing sorrow, there had been no replies. And in the end she had acknowledged defeat and given up any attempt to communicate.

But, to coincide with her stay in London, she had made one last attempt, and had written to them, to tell them she would be staying in Mount Street for a month, begging them to allow her to visit.

"Perhaps it was foolish of me to hope, Alicia," she concluded with a catch in her voice. "I can understand Papa's refusal to unbend—he was ever a high stickler, and Mama was firmly under his thumb. Even so, I cannot help but think how desperately lonely she must be . . . and to know she has grandchildren she will never see . . ."

"My dear, you must not distress yourself." The marchioness felt her own anger rising. It was iniquitous that Lord Welby should be permitted to inflict so much suffering on his own kith and kin. "One can hardly say that you have not tried. And your visit is too short to waste time brooding over 'might-have-beens.' "

It was perhaps fortunate that there were so many distractions. Most afternoons the ladies drove in Hyde Park at the fashionable hour. Here Lady Elizabeth was recognized by various members of the *haut ton*, and it gave Kate much pleasure to see in what affectionate regard her mother was still held by the majority of these doyens of society, despite her rejection of the pleasures life within such a society might have afforded her.

"Your dear mama has altered very little," exclaimed Lady Sefton, beaming at Kate as her carriage paused briefly alongside theirs in order to exchange pleasantries. "Why, you might almost be sisters."

Kate laughed. "I would be flattered if that were so, ma'am, but I will never be half as beautiful. My sister, Dierdre, is the lucky one. She is the image of Mama."

"Well, well, it is honest in you to say so, my dear." Lady Sefton smiled kindly. "But beauty does not lie in looks alone. You have clearly inherited Elizabeth's generous nature."

"I hardly knew how to reply," Kate later told Chloe as they walked beneath the spreading trees in company with many others. "To be honest, I still find such gushing compliments very difficult to take seriously."

"But then you seldom seem to take anything seriously."

"On the contrary, I take serious things very seriously, but all this . . ." She waved a hand.

Kate had been amazed and amused upon her first visit to Hyde Park during the so-called fashionable hour, between five and six o'clock, to discover how many people disported themselves in this manner. The green sward beneath the trees was transformed into a mass of swaying, shimmering color, the silks and muslins of the ladies mingling with pantalooned dandies sporting extravagant cravats and tight coats. And along the rides, fine carriages of all kinds, phaetons, both low- and high-perch—some dangerously high to her way of thinking—and curricules, as well as the more sober barouches and landaulets, carrying beautiful creatures of all ages and kinds. But it was all quite harmless and provided her with endless amusement, and the sun was pleasantly warm.

"I sometimes wish I had your ability to converse with anyone." Chloe's sigh was a touch rueful. "Mama is always exhorting me to cultivate the art of polite conversation. But I don't have your ease of manner. If someone pays me a compliment, I immediately react with blushing confusion."

"You are too hard on yourself, Chloe. For a start, you have a wonderful complexion, which is why you blush so delightfully. I, on the other hand, when embarrassed, turn crimson from the neck up, which is, I suppose, the penalty of having red hair."

"How can you think that a penalty!"

"It is, so. I also get freckles if the sun so much as touches my skin, which doesn't bother me one jot at home. But Lady St. Clair thinks them monstrous unfashionable, which is why I now cower beneath this parasol." She gave it an expert twirl.

"But, that's just it—you don't cower. You carry it with an air of exceeding elegance," Chloe insisted, to her friend's amusement, and then drew a sharp breath. "Kate, don't look now, but you will never guess who is coming toward us."

Kate, upon being told not to look, could never refrain from so doing. She therefore raised her eyes to see Blaise approaching them across the grass in company with Mr. Merivale. They had scarcely spoken since the night of the ball, and now, in defiance of all her fine resolutions to forget what had happened between them, her heart began to race and there was a ridiculous weakness in her knees. She drew a deep steadying breath and hoped that her parasol would lend her at least the appearance of cool composure. Since there was no way the gentlemen could be avoided, she clung to a determination to appear as light and free of care as she could manage.

It was Mr. Merivale who saw them first. He doffed his hat, drawing Blaise's attention to their presence.

"Here's a thing! Delighted to see you, dear young ladies. And looking quite charming, if I may be permitted to say so."

"You may indeed, kind sir," Kate returned, smiling warmly at him before making herself smile with equal ease at Blaise. For a moment their eyes locked, and she found his expression hard to read.

He wondered if she knew quite how desirable she looked as the breeze gusted strongly, molding the fine cream muslin of her gown to her figure; how, beneath the pretty ruched parasol, her eyes challenged him.

"I am amazed to see you taking the Grand Strut, Kate," he quizzed her, accepting the challenge. "Never tell me you are enjoying it?"

"Oh, but I am, Blaise. Quite prodigiously, in fact. I have discovered that it is, of all things, most important to be seen."

"And this from one who has always affected to despise such empty pleasures."

"That was before I realized how amusing they could be, once one learned not to take them seriously," she returned swiftly.

For a moment his eyes narrowed, as though uncertain whether he detected some particular barb concealed beneath the lightly spoken words.

"I hold that it is a great mistake to take anything seriously," said Mr. Merivale. "Except, of course, when one is dressing."

"But, of course," Kate agreed with mock seriousness.

"And I daresay you have received any number of invitations?"

"Indeed, yes. Dozens!" she agreed laughingly. "In truth, I am quite dizzy with it all. Not that I take any credit. If I had not had such an auspicious send-off from Grosvenor Square, with Lady St. Clair for my sponsor, and were I not my mother's daughter, things might have been very different."

"You are very cynical, of a sudden," Blaise said abruptly.

Kate stopped, with a defiant twirl of her parasol, her lively face upturned to him, while Mr. Merivale and Chloe looked on in silence, aware that there was more to the argument than mere words.

"Not at all. I am simply being realistic, as I have been from the start, if you remember." Her levity clearly displeased Blaise, for he frowned, though he did not attempt to argue with her or deny the truth of her words. "I suppose it comes from being but one of a large family, and I certainly have no fortune to commend me, which is in many ways what it is all about. But then, you know my views on that head. Nor am I a ravishing beauty, which just might obviate the need for a fortune."

"My dear Kate, you appear to hold a very low

opinion of society," Mr. Merivale said gently. "But not, I hope, of your friends?"

Kate turned impulsively to him. "Indeed, no! Friendships are to be treasured, and I would not have you think my words are in any way directed at you, my true friends. I am having a splendid time, and mean to make the very most of it. Lady Jersey has sent us vouchers for Almack's, whatever they are, and we are to go there before Mama and Papa go home. Everyone talks of it with hushed breath, but I have no idea what to expect. Is it very grand?"

"On the contrary," Blaise said with crushing sarcasm. "It is depressingly ordinary—little more than a hotbed for gossip and intrigue, in fact. The balls are dull in the extreme, the refreshments even duller—bread and butter and stale cakes—and nothing stronger than lemonade or tea."

A murmur of protest from Chloe, who was looking forward to her first visit with eager anticipation, was drowned by Kate's spontaneous gurgle of laughter.

"Good gracious! Yet everyone clamors to get in!"

"And may not do so without vouchers from the lady patronesses, of whom Lady Jersey is one. God only knows why they bother."

"Total exclusivity, dear boy," murmured Mr. Merivale. "Almack's is the high temple of the *ton*. One has but to put something out of bounds—and, *voilà*, it is the only place people wish to be. We all do it, and thus perpetuate the myth."

Kate laughed. "Extraordinary. I can hardly wait to see for myself."

When Lady St. Clair had boasted of being scarcely a night at home, she had spoken no less than the truth.

There were fetes and soirees, routs and balls, and

visits to the theater—the latter giving more pleasure to Kate than all the rest.

But all was not unmitigated gaiety, for as June advanced, so did the rumors that things were coming to a head across the Channel, and that a final confrontation with Bonaparte must come, sooner rather than later.

An air of tension descended upon the house in Mount Street. Dr. Sheridan took to scanning the pages of the *Times* over breakfast, his coffee turning cold as small grunts gave way to a disconcerting silence.

One morning, after they had been to Drury Lane to see Edmund Kean, whose quick, passionate energy had enchanted them all, Kate became aware that her father was more silent than usual. She and her mother exchanged glances. Lady Elizabeth said quietly, "Did you not enjoy the play, my love?"

"M'm? Oh, yes, very fine, very fine, indeed." He seemed to come back as from a great distance.

"Then, perhaps you are not feeling quite yourself. You have scarcely touched your breakfast."

He folded the paper with reluctance, and made only a perfunctory show of eating before pushing his plate aside, nodding to a servant who came at once to remove it.

"I have been thinking, Elizabeth, that I might travel to Brussels myself to find out exactly what's going on . . ."

There was general uproar as everyone tried to speak at once. Lady St. Clair set her cup down with a clatter, and Kate exclaimed, "Pa! You wouldn't? Not really?"

Her mother had turned very pale. "Patrick, you cannot! You must not. Why, I have heard that people are leaving Brussels like scared rabbits, and I daresay Lord Wellington is glad to see the back of them, with all he has on his plate—and here you are saying you want to go there! It would be madness! Only consider the danger!"

He ran a hand through the thatch of white hair already disarranged by restless fingers. "I have considered nothing else for days now, my dear, for it is a danger to which our son will inevitably be exposed."

"And don't I know that quite as well as you," she returned swiftly, her voice low and passionate. "But it is the life he has chosen . . . it is what he . . ." Her voice cracked. ". . . what he is paid to do. And besides, you have responsibilities—our other children to consider."

"I know that, right enough."

"Besides which, Pa," Kate said, recovering from the initial shock, and striving to be practical, "as Mama says, I doubt Lord Wellington would want people cluttering the place up."

"He might be glad of an extra doctor, however, if battle is joined."

The words dropped into a deafening silence.

After which everyone spoke at once. Dr. Sheridan waited, head bowed, until they had exhausted all the arguments. Then he took his wife's trembling hands in a firm, yet gentle clasp.

"I cannot simply stand aside, my dear."

She gave a deep shuddering sigh, all thought of breakfast banished. He took her trembling hand in his own. "I cannot be so close and stand aside, my dear. You must see that."

Admiration and fear struggled for supremacy as Kate watched her mother bow her head in assent. "I know that once you have an idea in your head, nothing will shift it."

"Patrick, this is madness!" exclaimed the marchioness. "Kit chose to be a soldier, and is therefore bound to do his duty, but your first duty is surely to the rest of your family—to Elizabeth . . ." But she was already talking to the air, and she knew it. "Oh, well, if you must, I believe Blaise has some high-up connections at Horseguards. He can probably arrange with them to cut a few corners. And Dominic might also be able to use his influence, with his Foreign Office cronies."

After that everything seemed to happen very quickly—too quickly, for all too soon, Lady Elizabeth was packing a small portmanteau, putting on a brave face as Kate had seen her do so many times with Kit.

And then Blaise was at the door with his traveling chaise, good-byes were hastily completed, and then Dr. Sheridan was gone. And only then, just for a moment, did Lady Elizabeth's composure crack. Kate put an arm around her trembling shoulders.

"Pa will be all right, Mama," she said, with more assurance than she felt.

"Of course he will, my dear." Lady Elizabeth straightened her shoulders, dabbed her eyes with a handkerchief, and attempted a smile. "Men! They are all alike. Overgrown boys, ever ready to court danger. I should be used to it by now, but your father has never until now displayed . . ." She gave her shoulders a little fatalistic shrug. "He is by far too sensible, I am sure, to behave rashly."

And too caring to spare himself, if the need arose, Kate realized with a heavy heart, but she kept the thought to herself.

# Fourteen

It seemed extraordinary to Kate that, with a battle that could affect all their lives imminent, life could simply carry on as normal, with parties and balls the order of the day.

"Does no one care?" Kate demanded of Blaise as they took one of their early morning rides on the day following her father's departure.

"That rather depends. For the vast majority of people who are hell-bent on pleasure and have no personal involvement, I suppose their idea of war is of some kind of heroic pageant in which our brave soldiers will naturally triumph. Also, it is happening a long way away, and therefore has little or nothing to do with their world."

"How selfish!"

He half-smiled. "Perhaps. But they would deny any such sentiment vehemently if you charged them with it, and profess themselves to be patriotic."

Blaise had returned from seeing her father safely aboard a ship carrying troops bound for Belgium, assuring Lady Elizabeth that he had left her husband in good spirits. Kate thought he seemed subdued, and determined that as soon as she could speak to him alone, she would demand to know the truth. Her chance came on that same morning.

"You believe I would lie to you?"

"No." She hesitated, for there had been a tautness in his voice that belied the words. "But you might well conceal some unpleasant facts which you believed it might be preferable that Mama did not know."

He shot her a wry look. "Oh, Kate, you are by far too perceptive."

"So there is something?"

His hands tightened momentarily on the rein and his horse jinked. "Not in the way of hard facts. But there is a feeling that matters are moving inexorably toward a final reckoning."

"In other words, a battle is imminent?"

He uttered an abrupt laugh. "You are a great one for plain speaking, Kate. Very well, then—yes, a battle is imminent. In fact—and this is for your ears only—it has already begun." He heard her draw in a sharp breath. "The most recently received dispatches reveal that Wellington has, in his own words, been 'humbugged.' It seems that Napoleon stole a march on him while he was at a ball given by Lady Richmond . . ."

"A ball, at such a time!"

His mouth twisted wryly. "Extraordinary as it may seem, it was held with his permission—or so I was told. Seemingly, he thought to reassure people, thereby averting panic, believing as he undoubtedly did that time would be on his side. But the French began to move sooner than he had expected."

Kate felt a crawling sensation in the pit of her stomach, for now there was not only Kit to worry about. "Will Pa be safe in Brussels?"

"I'm sure he will." Blaise thought it better she should not know that people were even now pouring out of Brussels at an alarming rate, desperate to take ship for England and safety. Though everyone would know soon enough.

"But you will tell me—if you hear anything, anything at all?" She met his searching glance, unaware how desperate was the mute pleading in her eyes. "Mama is a very strong person, and if something were to happen to Kit . . ." her voice faltered, "I think she might just be able to bear it. But she and Pa . . ." Kate paused, then continued, "if anything were to befall Pa, and she was not there, I believe it would break her spirit as well as her heart."

Blaise was silent, remembering how his own tragedy had almost cost him his reason. And Lucinda had been part of him for so short a time by comparison.

"Let us hope it will not come to that," he said. And then, unexpectedly, "Your mother is fortunate to have you for a daughter."

Kate felt the color flood into her cheeks. "I suppose we have always been a close-knit family." To cover her embarrassment she said, "May we gallop, do you think? There is no one about."

It seemed to Kate that their ride that morning signified a subtle change in their relationship. Since the evening of the ball, and the incident which had transformed her own feelings in an instant, she had formed the definite impression that Blaise had been avoiding her. Yet, despite the fact that she had early rejected any lingering illusions concerning his feelings for her, there was a perceptible softening in his manner, to which she instinctively responded, born though it inevitably must be, of sympathy.

Her mama had been quite adamant that life must go on as planned in spite of events. Staying at home with long faces would, she insisted, serve no purpose except to make everyone feel twice as miserable.

And then a diversion occurred which gave their thoughts another direction. Blaise had received a letter from Miss Glynn later on that same day, informing him that Freddie had a severe toothache, and requesting his permission to bring the children up to Town to visit the dentist.

"Oh, poor Freddie," Kate exclaimed, a sentiment that was echoed by Miss Priddy to the accompaniment of much sighing.

"He'll get over it," said his unsympathetic father. "A few days in Town will more than compensate for any discomfort."

"How heartless," Kate chided him.

"Not at all." His accompanying smile made him look momentarily very like his son.

"You will, of course, go down to Kimberley yourself to fetch them," said Lady St. Clair. "Poor Miss Glynn will have her hands more than full if Freddie is in pain."

"You are right, I suppose." His brows came down, and, so casually as to appear almost as an afterthought, "A pity you cannot accompany me, Kate. You are so very good with the children."

In spite of all her good intentions, Kate's heart leapt. But before she could answer, he added wryly, "It wouldn't do, of course. The gabble grinders would seize upon such behavior with great glee, and your reputation would be ruined."

Kate collected herself, swallowed her disappointment and the urge to say "Let them!"

The marchioness exchanged meaningful glances with Elizabeth. They both cherished hopes that something might come of the growing accord between Blaise and Kate. Nevertheless, both were also obliged to agree that it would not do.

"Perhaps, if I were to accompany you . . . as a kind of chaperone," Miss Priddy offered diffidently and quite unexpectedly, and blushed when they all turned to look at her.

"My dear Priddy," said the marchioness. "It is very kind of you to offer, but I fear you would find my son's pace quite beyond you. When Blaise travels, he does not stay for anyone."

"Oh . . . I see. Of course . . ." Miss Priddy blushed furiously and said in embarrassed confusion, "Well then, perhaps . . . I rather think . . ."

"And, in any case," added the marchioness, to put her out of her misery, though reluctantly, for it would have been an excellent way to bring the two young people she most cared for together, "we are promised to Lady Cowper's soiree this evening, and she would be most disappointed if Kate were not there."

"Well, that settles the matter. I had better be off," the marquess said abruptly. "The sooner I go, the sooner Freddie will be put out of his misery."

That night at the soiree, Charlie Stanford attached himself to Kate with increasing tenacity. His eagerness grated on her rather more than usual, but there was little she could do about it without appearing rude, though she was a little short with him more than once.

"Feeling a trifle under par, are we, m'dear?" he asked oversolicitously when she had snapped at him for the second time. "Too many balls and the like, I daresay, what?"

"You are probably right." She found his patronizing manner deeply offensive, but bit back the urge to tell him so, and forced a smile. "Also, we are all a little worried at present—about Pa, and my brother."

"What? Ah, yes. Dr. Sheridan has gone out to Brussels, too, so Uncle Charles tells me. But I shouldn't worry your pretty head about all this talk of war, m'dear. If it comes to blows, Lord Wellington'll soon see off that petty tyrant, Bonaparte."

Kate found his dismissive attitude more than a little insulting, not simply to her, but to those troops, Kit among them, who could even now be in the thick of battle. She longed to tell him so, but was obliged to bite on her tongue in order not to betray how much she knew.

"Is that young pup getting serious about Kate?" Sir Dominic asked of Lady St. Clair. As a connoisseur of people's characters, he watched the two young people with interest. "Can't imagine she'll have him. Too addle-pated for an intelligent young woman like Kate."

Lady St. Clair laughed. "There's no harm in Charlie, but I totally agree with you. However, I am confident that there is little danger of her taking him seriously."

"Should have thought Blaise might fancy his chances. Any interest there? They'd make a fine pair."

"Oh, Dominic, it is Elizabeth's dearest wish as well as mine," she confided with a sigh. "But I cannot make them out. They did not get on at all well when first they met, for Kate was not slow to speak her mind, and he thought her much too coming. But perhaps that was exactly what he needed to release him from the memory of Lucinda, for there have been moments recently when I have wondered . . . but I am probably air-dreaming."

"Ah, well, the young were ever contrary. Now, you and I, Alicia, understand one another perfectly."

"Do we?" She became confused and colored quite delightfully, making him smile, she thought, rather like the cat who had been at the cream pot.

Across the room, someone else was watching Kate—a very beautiful dark-eyed young woman in a lilac gown cut daringly low. At first Kate thought she was imagining her interest, but finally she asked Chloe if she knew who the woman was.

Chloe followed her gaze and looked away

quickly. "Lud! It's Mrs. Broughton. I had not thought to see her here."

"Should the name convey something to me?"

"She is a widow, fearfully rich, so I remember Mama saying." Chloe giggled. "She was Lord St. Clair's mistress for a while, seen everywhere on his arm. Mama reckoned she was desperate to become more than his inamorata, but he tired of her and turned her off . . ." She became aware that her companion had gone very quiet, and that Kate's smile had a set look. "It was before you came to Town, of course."

Kate made some trite comment, and felt a little sick.

"Does no one in this so-wonderful society world think and talk of anything but scandal?" she demanded angrily of Mr. Merivale, meeting him a few minutes later.

He wondered what had brought about such an uncharacteristic outburst, but only said with a faint smile, "I fear we must on the whole appear a sorry lot, m'dear. It's a kind of game we play, d'ye see. But there is no real harm in most of us."

"Oh, I am sorry," she exclaimed, mortified. "I wasn't referring to you, Mr. Merivale. How could you think I would accuse you when I account you my friend."

His smile deepened. "I daresay I am no different from the rest, but you are kind to reassure me." He paused, then said, "Do you think you might call me Gervase? Then I shall know I am truly your friend."

"Thank you. I should like that." Her eyes warmed and she wondered whether to tell him the whole and ask him for the truth about Mrs. Broughton, but decided that she would rather not know. "And I am sorry I took out my frustration on you," she said. "I find it so difficult, you see, to be light-hearted when . . ."

"Quite. A worrying time." Though that ain't what's eating at you, he thought.

He had noted Amelia Broughton's presence, and her look of bitterness as she had watched Kate, and hoped that no one would see fit to enlighten Kate about the young widow's involvement with his friend.

"Blaise has gone down to Kimberley, I'm told. That young rip of his has the toothache."

"Yes. Poor Freddie. But at his age the pain is soon forgotten. We will have to think of some special treat to speed his recovery."

"Astley's Amphitheater, perhaps?" suggested Mr. Merivale. "It is, I believe, exactly the kind of entertainment to take a child's mind off unpleasant things."

"Of course. How clever you are. Perhaps you might even care to accompany them?"

He shuddered, and begged to be excused. And she laughed at him, feeling suddenly much brighter.

The children arrived soon after midday on the following day, tired and fretful. Freddie's cheek was red and swollen, though he was making an effort to be brave, and they both managed a wan smile for their grandmother and Kate, who had gone to Grosvenor Square to await their arrival.

It was Kate who took Freddie to the dentist later that afternoon, Miss Glynn being noticeably worn to a thread. She was gracious enough to admit, in tones bordering on disbelief, that the marquess had endeavored from time to time to engage Freddie's interest with heroic tales of daring-do—some of which she had obviously thought quite unsuitable for a small boy, and would probably give him nightmares—but it was she who had endured the brunt of trying to pacify the two fretful children throughout what was a very long journey, and without the comfort of Cormac, for their father had firmly insisted that the dog would dislike the journey, and must stay at Kimberley.

Freddie survived the dentist with great stoicism, and after a good night's sleep, aided by a weak dose of laudanum, was almost back to his old self. His only sadness was having to leave Cormac at home.

"He is grown 'normously, Kate," he chattered away happily, when Miss Glynn took Roseanne off to rest, "and he almost always does as he's told. He remembered Papa, too, and licked his face . . ." Kate smiled involuntarily, picturing the scene. "And I can ride my pony, Cherry, without a leading rein, now. Kenny says I am a nat'ral-born horseman."

"It would seem that my son is well on the way to recovery," drawled the marquess, coming in as the boy was in full flow. "What it is to be young."

Kate started, not having heard him come into the room. She said, not quite looking at him, "Children are surprisingly resilient."

"So it would seem," he said dryly. "Apropos of that, I believe that you and Gervase have been plotting behind my back, Kate."

Kate frowned, and then remembered. "Oh, yes . . . the . . ."

"How could you think it the kind of place I would wish to visit, let alone agree to do so, especially with an excitable child in tow?" he reproached her, making her laugh.

"Two children, surely," she insisted. "It would be most unkind in you to leave one behind."

He winced. "Kate! I beg of you!"

"Oh, come now! A few hours . . . surely you would not begrudge a few hours . . ." She saw that

Freddie was looking from one to the other, puzzled.

"You're a hard woman, Kate Sheridan," he said with something like despair, though there was a glint in his eyes. "My reputation is like to be ruined, for I shall be a butt for every wit and joke-smith in town." And when she showed no sign of relenting, "Oh, very well, then. But on one condition. That you come too."

They went two days later to the Royal Amphitheater in Lambeth, with Pogson up on the box, hardly able to contain a grin of pure amusement at the thought of his lordship frequenting such a venue, let alone playing the unaccustomed role of father for the second time within a week.

For Freddie, it was a joyful experience from beginning to end, with performing monkeys, trick riding, and comical clowns; Roseanne was a bit apprehensive at first and inclined to be tearful, but she too was soon captivated by the sight of a fairy-like lady dancing on the back of a beautiful white horse, and thereafter enjoyed the pantomime and the songs.

The marquess watched their faces and then turned his attention to Kate, who was pointing out to his daughter the tumblers who were at that moment entering the circus ring, performing amazing acrobatics to the applause of the crowd. There was such a wealth of tenderness about her that for an instant the noise of the crowd receded and he was aware only of her, and of the tumultuous thudding of his own heart.

# Fifteen

London was a'buzz with rumor.

For days now ships had been disgorging passengers fleeing from Brussels. The roads to the Belgian coast, it was rumored, had been choked with carriages of every kind, some carrying soldiers wounded in battle. There were lurid tales of death and dreadful injuries inflicted by the French, and of the imminence of defeat.

Everyone knew by now that a great and final battle had been joined at a place called Waterloo. And all but a stubborn few feared the worst.

"My money is still on Wellington," said the marquess, as he sat watching Gervase discard yet another cravat in his effort to achieve a perfect waterfall.

"Well, I hope you may be proved right, dear boy," murmured Mr. Merivale, selecting another length of white linen from several adorning the arm of his manservant, Giles. "I have no desire to pass the rest of my days under the heel of some pettyfogging little Corsican upstart. There . . ." He carefully pressed the last crease into place and stood up. "A tolerable achievement, I believe."

"Poseur!" scoffed the marquess.

"Not at all." Giles carefully inserted him into his latest blue superfine, and adjusted the high collar. "One has a duty to one's tailor, dear boy."

"Yet another new fellow, by the look of it."

"The last one threatened to dun me, would you believe?" Mr. Merivale drawled, and, catching his friend's quizzical eye, said in his droll way, "Can't have that."

"How much did you owe him, Gervase?"

"Oh, some trifling amount. It don't signify." He tucked his snuff box into a pocket designed to take it, and said in quite a different voice, "Is there any news of Kate's father or brother?"

"As yet, no. If there is still no word tomorrow, I mean to go across to Brussels myself."

Mr. Merivale opened his sleepy eyes. "A trifle risky, ain't it, dear old fellow?"

"Perhaps. But, although Lady Elizabeth is bearing up well, the strain of it is costing her dear."

"And Kate?" he asked casually.

There was a protracted silence. Then: "Oh, you know Kate. She is being optimistic for her mother's sake, but she is growing more tense with every day that passes."

Which is why you talk of going to Brussels, though you would emphatically deny it, thought Mr. Merivale.

"It's a bad business," he said.

The following morning, Blaise took Kate aside.

"I don't want you to say anything to anyone, Kate, but I am going to Horseguards this morning, and if I get no satisfactory answers, I mean to take ship for Belgium, to find out for myself what is happening."

The color left her face, leaving it alarmingly pale.

"Blaise, you can't! You must not! It would be terribly dangerous." She clutched at his arm to reinforce her argument.

He gently pried her fingers loose, but continued

to hold her hand, his eyes never leaving her face. "And would that matter so much to you?"

"Well, of course it would!" She stopped, bit her lip, and tried to recover herself, but a tide of guilty color had already overwhelmed her pallor. "After all, my family can hardly be considered your problem," she concluded lamely.

He was silent for a long moment. Then he said harshly, "You think not? When I see you daily growing more distraught, and trying gallantly to hide it from your mama? Oh, Kate!"

Her heart began to thud, for in a moment she was certain he would kiss her. But instead the door opened, and Lady St. Clair was saying urgently, "Blaise—Grayson told me you were here. Is there news?"

Belatedly, she took in the significance of the scene before her, but already Blaise was moving away from Kate with a warning glance, saying smoothly, "Nothing as yet, Mama. I am just on my way to discover if there are any fresh developments."

"I hope there may be something soon. I fear that poor Elizabeth is beginning to prepare herself for the worst."

"Tell her not to lose heart," he said briefly. And, nodding to them both, quit the room, leaving Kate with a curious sensation of loss.

But he was back within the hour as they were about to sit down to luncheon, though no one had much appetite. There was a sense of urgency about his step.

"Something has happened." Lady Elizabeth was steadied by her daughter. She was white-faced, and seemed to have aged years in a few days.

"They are safe and on their way," he said quietly, and saw her sway.

"Ah! Thanks be to God!"

Kate echoed the sentiment, but her joy was tempered by the hint of something more in his voice.

"Safe, you say?" she demanded.

His coattails swung around as he turned to lay down his hat and gloves on a small side table. Kate sensed that he was buying time in order to choose his words.

"Your husband is very tired, but unharmed, Lady Elizabeth," he began.

There was a tiny echoing silence. Then: "Kit?" she whispered, seeing from his face that there was more.

"Has lost an arm, and still has a bullet lodged in his left leg . . ." There was a concerted gasp, as he quietly continued, "but he has come through well, and should make a good recovery. Dr. Sheridan is with him at present, but will come to you as soon as he feels able to leave Kit in good hands."

Kate pictured her brother, never still, never happier than when he was riding or shooting, or fighting his battles. "Oh, poor Kit!" she whispered.

Lady Elizabeth looked at St. Clair piteously for a moment, her eyes brilliant, as though afraid to believe. Then suddenly she slumped in a faint.

"Mama!" Kate cried.

"Oh, my dearest Elizabeth!" exclaimed Lady St. Clair, hurrying to her friend's side, her smelling bottle in hand. "It is but the shock of relief," she reassured Kate as her mother began to stir, moaning a little. "She has born the waiting so bravely, and refused all offers of laudanum to help her sleep. Now she will surely not refuse it." Her ladyship looked to her son. "Do you think you could carry her upstairs? She will be able to sleep in the knowledge that those she loves are safe, and that all will be well."

When Blaise came downstairs, Kate was staring

out of the window. She turned as he came into the room.

"How bad is Kit, truly?" Her voice cracked, then firmed as her eyes challenged him. "I am not a fool, so I know it is worse than you said. You need not spare me."

Blaise looked at her for a moment without speaking. "He is appallingly weak from loss of blood and the shock of the amputation." He saw her flinch, but her gaze held steady. "Also the bullet is in an awkward place and will present difficulties in its removal." He hesitated before concluding, "At the moment it is best left alone, but your father is confident of being able to remove it as soon as his general condition improves."

"Can I see him?"

"Presently." Blaise thought of the indescribable chaos he had so recently left. It was no place for a gently bred young woman, even one possessed of Kate's exceptional qualities. "I could not condone your visiting him at present, nor indeed would they permit it." Blaise walked across to a chiffonier, where a brandy decanter and glasses reposed. He poured two measures, one small and a larger one for himself. "Sit down and drink it," he said. And when Kate protested that she was not so poorspirited as to have need of it, his voice hardened. "Do as I say. It will make you feel better, I promise."

So she sat at one end of the sofa, perched on its edge, and as she reluctantly sipped the fiery liquid, he continued, "The hospital housing him is, as you may imagine, in a state of mayhem. It is therefore my intention, as soon as he can be moved, to have him brought to Grosvenor Square, where he will have peace and quiet. And there, as soon as your father thinks the time is right, he will himself undertake to remove the bullet."

"How like Pa to insist!" She attempted a smile, though her green eyes were liquid-bright with unshed tears. "It will not be easy for him, but I know he would not have it any other way." She hesitated, then continued, "It is very kind of you to offer your home . . ."

"Kind?" He said the word as though it were foreign to him. He seldom thought of his house as a home, but more as the place where he lived. "Kindness hardly comes into it, for there is room enough and to spare," he added stiffly. He saw that she looked suddenly weary. "However, all that may be arranged later. Go now and rest, Kate," he said, drawing her to her feet. "All will be well, I promise you."

And sure enough, within a matter of days, Kit was brought to Grosvenor Square, amid the continuing gaiety of a rejoicing nation and the echoing chimes of church bells ringing out to celebrate a great victory.

Kate and her mother were there to meet him, and see him settled in a suite of rooms set aside for him. Kate was secretly appalled to see how frail he looked, his rich auburn hair dirty and disheveled, his face bloodless and rough with stubble, but his eyes were bright, perhaps too bright, and his spirit was undimmed as he caught her hand.

"We did it, little sister," he murmured with a wide grin. "Finished Boney once and for all."

"You did, indeed," she agreed, trying not to look at his empty sleeve. But, weak as he was, her distress did not escape him.

"Oh, don't let that worry you. I shall manage very well without it. And once Pa has removed that damned bullet from my leg, I shall soon be as good as new." He winced a little as they endeavored to make him comfortable. "I'll be back with the regiment before you know it."

"Kit! You cannot be serious?" cried his mother. "Surely you will not think of such a thing."

Kate said nothing, for it was quite clear to her that it would be impossible, but he guessed the train of her thoughts and grinned weakly.

"I'm not finished, Kate, girl. Far from it. Can't let Boney triumph, can we? Take more than a few trifling injuries to stop me. Did Pa tell you—the Duke visited me before I left Brussels? Wasn't that splendid of him? He told me I'm to be made up to major, and as soon as I'm fit, he has promised me a place on his staff."

He was clearly becoming flushed and feverish. "That is splendid news, Kit, but you must rest now if you wish to get better, and here is Pa come to see that you do as you are told."

An anxious few days followed as Dr. Sheridan fought to contain the fever, caused partly by the bullet wound which, from being roughly bound on the field of battle, was showing a tendency to fester, and required regular fomentations to bring it under control. Lady Elizabeth, once over the shock, became her old practical self and bore the brunt of the nursing, having roundly rejected any attempt to bring in a nurse from outside.

"A poor thing it would be," she protested, "an' I were to let some stranger tend my dear boy."

Kate visited daily to allow her to rest, and her father was seldom far away. Kate, when she was not otherwise engaged, relieved Miss Glynn by taking the children out to the park, for in the unsettled conditions it had proven almost impossible to keep to a strict regime.

"Freddie is at an inquiring age," she explained to Blaise. "He is longing to see the hero who lost his arm."

"Little beast!"

"Not at all. Little boys are almost invariably pos-

sessed of a ghoulish curiosity. I speak as one who
has grown up with three brothers."

She continued to surprise him with her wisdom
and common-sense. His eyebrow quirked, and he
said, though without enthusiasm, "I suppose I
should take them back to Kimberley."

"Oh, that would be a pity. All kinds of celebrations are being planned, and it would be such a
pity were they to miss them." She appeared to hesitate. "May I make a suggestion?" she ventured.
"Now that my parents are here almost perma-
nently, could the children and Miss Glynn not come
to Mount Street? That way, they wouldn't be under
anyone's feet. I'm sure your mother would not object and I know Ellen would love to help Miss
Glynn to look after them."

He eyed her with a mixture of awe and amusement. "Have you always had this propensity for or-
ganizing other people's lives?"

She colored faintly. "I suppose I have a fairly
practical mind. When one is the eldest girl in a
fairly large and boisterous family, it becomes something of a prerequisite if any kind of order is to be
maintained."

How dull it sounded put into words. But he did
not seem to think it so, for he was still regarding
her quizzically. "So, you think my mother wouldn't
mind?"

"I'm sure she wouldn't. You know how she adores
the children."

And, when asked, Lady St. Clair was delighted
to agree. "It will be so much better all around. They
will be away from any reminders of the sick room,
and I'm sure Jameson will not be sorry to see the
back of them, good as they are." A sudden smile lit
up her face—something Kate hadn't seen for days.
"Though I dare not hazard what Grayson will
make of them."

# Sixteen

London was again *en fete*, though not perhaps with the abandon of the previous summer.

"There are crowds everywhere," Kate told Kit when she visited him.

She did not add that there were also an increasing number of soldiers wandering the streets, many of them looking weary and somehow lost.

Kit was making good progress. The stump of his arm was healing well, and Dr. Sheridan had finally been able to remove the bullet from his thigh—a tricky operation, during which he had been aided, surprisingly, by the marquess, who dismissed his part as minimal and scarcely worthy of mention.

"I merely did what was asked of me," he said. "No special skill was required."

"You are too modest, my lord," said the doctor. "I have had many a trainee surgeon pass out cold when required to hold a limb steady during just such a delicate operation."

Kate stared at him in amazement. "You did that?"

Her question seemed to irk him. "It was not exactly heroic. Perhaps I am simply not possessed of overmuch delicacy of feeling."

Kate glanced at her father, whose look urged her not to press the matter. She did not see so much of Blaise in the days that followed, as the children took up more of her time when she was not with Kit. Ellen had been obliged to go home. Her mother had been taken ill, and she was needed to look after the family. Grayson was not too happy with the arrangement, but Mrs. Gibson said, "Of course Ellen must go; we will manage."

There was little doubt that two children in the house did make a lot of extra work, but although the situation was not entirely to Miss Glynn's liking, she kept them out of the way as much as she could, and it seemed to Kate that she was the only one to be inconvenienced by Ellen's absence.

It was Joss who came to fetch her—a very different Joss than the one Kate remembered. So different that she did not immediately recognize him as she left to take the children for a walk and found him kicking his heels outside waiting for Ellen to collect her things. For one thing, he was clean, his hair still black and curly but neatly trimmed, and his clothes, though shabby, were also clean as well as being practical. He seemed to have grown several inches, and although the air of jaunty assurance was still apparent, it was no longer defensive.

"You are very good with the horses, so Ellen tells me," she said.

"Yeh." He gave her a cheeky grin. "Got a nat'ral affinity wiv 'em, so 'is nibs' says."

"What do you do?" Freddie asked, impressed by the boy's assurance.

"Gor' blimey, all kinds of fings," he said airily. "Stokin' the furnace, an' groomin' the 'orses. An' I can almost shoe an' 'orse on me own now."

"I'd like to see that. I have a pony at home," Freddie continued in his friendly way. "He's called Cherry. You'd like him."

"I 'spect I would." Joss sniffed. "I gits ter ride the 'orses 'ccasionally."

"I've got a ball. P'raps we could play sometime?"

"Well, I dunno. I'm busy most times, see, cos it's an important job I got."

"Oh, well . . ." Freddie shrugged philosophically. "P'raps we'll come to see you sometime. Can we, Kate?"

Kate tried to imagine Blaise's reaction if asked the same question—and knew what the answer would be. Thankfully, Ellen appeared at that moment with her few things wrapped in a bundle.

"I feel real bad, leaving you like this, Miss Kate. But Mam must be poorly or she'd never have sent for me."

"I know that, Ellen." Out of the corner of her eye, Kate saw Joss hopping impatiently from foot to foot. "But we'll manage. You get along, now. Goodbye, Joss."

"Bye, missus."

"I wish I could nearly shoe a horse," Freddie said wistfully. "Joss is nice, isn't he?"

Kate murmured agreement and subtly directed his mind into other channels. She had thought it prudent not to mention Joss, but she reckoned without Freddie who, despite Miss Glynn's obvious disapproval, was full of their brief encounter when his father came around later that afternoon and found them together in the drawing room.

"I trust you don't mean to encourage my son's predilection for mingling with the riff and raff," he said with deceptive mildness when Miss Glynn had carried the protesting boy off to get ready for their afternoon walk.

"As if I would," Kate returned lightly. "Though I firmly believe that it does children no harm to learn that there are others less fortunate than themselves."

"As long as that is all it teaches them," he said, giving her a sanguine look. "I doubt my mother

would care for it if he were to come out with 'Gor'
blimey' in front of her friends."

"Oh, no!" Kate tried to keep a straight face and
failed as she gave way to a trill of laughter. "Why
must children always pick up on the very thing
they should not. My young brothers are just as bad.
Joss was only here for a few moments."

"A few moments, seemingly, is all it takes."

"Yes. Well, I'm sorry, but I doubt Joss will have
occasion to come again."

She did not sound in the least contrite, but he
was so diverted by the way the laughter lit up her
eyes that he refrained from pursuing the matter.

"Have you seen Kit today? Father is very pleased
with his progress."

"Your brother appears to be in excellent spirits.
When I looked in on him this afternoon, I found
young Chloe Melchester keeping him entertained."

"Was she, indeed? I could not be more pleased. I
had hoped that they might become good friends,
for now that he is so much better, I know how frus-
trated Kit will become with his continuing inactiv-
ity. And Chloe's easy chatter is just the thing to
divert him."

"I trust you do not mean to add matchmaking to
your many accomplishments—at least not while
Kit is under my roof."

"I would not presume," she said primly. "In any
case, Mama will not be far away, and even if she
were not, knowing Lady Melchester as I do, she
will have insisted upon Chloe's maid accompanying her as chaperone."

"Maids can be persuaded to look the other way."

Kate's trill of laughter set the corners of his own
mouth twitching. "Goodness, Blaise! I had no idea
you were so knowledgeable in assessing the devi-
ous ways of maids."

"My dear girl," he said, moving closer, "there are a great many things you don't know about me."

He had called her his "dear girl" as if he meant it. Her pulse began to race and her cheeks grew warm. In another moment he might take her in his arms.

"Ah, there you are, my dears." Lady St. Clair came hurrying in, and the moment was gone, leaving Kate feeling quite ridiculously bereft. She stole a glance at Blaise, but his face as usual gave nothing away.

Belatedly, Lady St. Clair realized that she had chosen an inopportune moment, but having done so, she had no option but to continue with her mission.

"Grayson told me I should find you here, Blaise. I wished to ask whether or not you mean to go to Lady Chessington's celebration ball tomorrow evening."

"Why do you ask?"

"I wondered if you might care to take us in your carriage. I could then offer Elizabeth and Patrick the use of mine. They are promised to a doctor friend of Patrick's and it would not do for them to be hiring a common hack."

"Well, whether I go or not, you may have one of mine and welcome. It would appear that everyone in London is holding some special victory ball, or breakfast, or the like."

"Yes, isn't it splendid?" said his mother happily.

"Is it?" To alleviate his unaccountable feeling of restlessness he strode to the window and pulled back the curtain to look down. "To tell the truth, I am fast growing weary of celebrating. We had a surfeit of it last year, which turned out to be more than a little premature. I only hope to God we are not in danger of making the same mistake again."

"You are in a mood, Blaise," his mother protested.

"I am quite sure those in charge will not allow that man to escape a second time. And, as for the rest of us, you surely would not deny people the opportunity to express their pleasure and relief at so great a victory."

"And even greater loss of life," said her son unequivocally. "To say nothing of the poor devils maimed and destitute. I doubt they feel much like celebrating."

"Blaise, this is not like you." His mother glanced keenly at his rigid back. "Are you unwell?"

He swung around with an abrupt laugh. "No, Mama, just blue-deviled—what Freddie would call glumpish. Take no notice of me."

"Perhaps if you spent more time with Freddie, he might give your thoughts a happier direction," Kate suggested, in an endeavor to tease him into a happier frame of mind. "Kit thinks he is very bright for his age. Apparently they have been discussing Wellington's strategy at Waterloo, and Kit was quite impressed with his quick grasp of some of the finer points."

"The sooner that young rip goes back to Kimberley, the better. He is in serious danger of being spoiled, to say nothing of having his head filled with dangerous trivia."

She was taken aback. "Blaise, you would not be so cruel as to send him home now when he is really enjoying himself."

The note of censure in her voice merely served to aggravate him the more. "I may very well do so. And I am surprised to find you encouraging this latest interest," he said austerely. "To say nothing of your brother's participation—in view of his recent harrowing experience."

She uttered a little trill of laughter. "Oh, but Kit is quite as enthusiastic as Freddie. They have been having a great time making paper models of the gun placements—at least, Freddie has made most of them—so they can act out the various maneuvers."

"Good God!" he exclaimed with an abrupt laugh. "Your brother is clearly as irrepressible as my son." He turned toward the door. "But I warn you, it will have to stop. I will not have Kit filling Freddie's head with tales that make soldiering seem splendid and heroic—and, worst of all, fun."

"As if he would!" Kate was incensed, and rushed to the defense of her beloved brother. "Kit may seem lightminded to you, Blaise, but he is not irresponsible. Far from it, for he would never seek to influence young minds, and is always very careful what he says when Calum and Michael are within hearing."

"But then, in your eyes, Kit can do no wrong," said the marquess, opening the door and closing it behind him with a decided snap.

Well, thought his mother with considerable interest, one might almost think him to be jealous of Kate's fondness for her brother.

The following afternoon Kate was in the unusual position of finding herself alone for a while. Lady St. Clair had been carried off by Sir Dominic to some diplomatic function, her parents were visiting friends, and Miss Glynn had taken the children out for their walk. Even Miss Priddy was out, having recently rediscovered a friend of earlier days.

"I could scarcely believe my eyes," she had told them all at dinner last evening, her nerves less evident, and her cheeks quite pink with excitement.

"There I was in the circulating library, dear Lady St. Clair, trying to decide between a volume of Alexander Pope's poetry and that new novel which has received such favorable reviews, when who should come in but Miss Almeria Payne. I had not

seen her since our schooldays, but there was no
mistaking her, for she has quite a prominent nose,
you know. Poor Almeria . . . she was teased quite
unmercifully at the time, I remember, though she
took it all in good part. We had such a jolly chat,
and she has asked me to take tea with her at her little house in Pimlico . . . if you have no objections,
that is . . ."

"My dear Priddy, of course you must go," Lady
St. Clair had said, repressing a smile. "I am delighted that you have rediscovered an old friend."

Kate was not sorry to have a little time to herself.
Life had become one long round of parties, visits,
and balls, and much as she was enjoying it, a brief
respite was very welcome. She did wonder if she
ought to visit Kit, but it was highly probable that
Chloe would be there, and she had no wish to play
gooseberry.

While she was still debating what to do with her
moment of freedom, Grayson came to say that
there was a lady below, asking to see her mama.

"I told her that Lady Elizabeth was out for the afternoon, Miss Kate, but as the news seemed to distress her, and she seemed a trifle frail, I took the
liberty of suggesting that she might care to see you
instead." Grayson hesitated.

"Did the lady not give her name, Grayson?"

"She seemed loath to do so, Miss Kate. But her
carriage does bear a crest."

Intrigued, she told him to show the lady up.
"And tea, I think, don't you?"

She came hesitantly into the room, clutching her
reticule, a small pale-faced elderly lady in black
bombazine, unfashionably cut, her bonnet neat and
trimmed with lace. She halted, staring at Kate with
a curious intensity, and suddenly seemed to go
paler still and sway a little.

Kate hurried forward and put an arm about her. "Dear ma'am, do, pray, take a seat."

She settled her into a comfortable chair and stood back, unsure how to proceed. "You wished to see my mama, I believe," she began.

"You must be Kate," the woman said in a trembling voice. "How like Elizabeth . . ." She stopped, fumbled in her reticule, and retrieved a handkerchief, which she pressed to her mouth.

Realization dawned upon Kate with startling suddenness. "And you are my grandmother!" For undoubtedly it was she. All the indignation and anger she had felt on her mama's behalf melted away as she was faced with this frail creature who seemed on the verge of collapse.

"I had to come," Lady Welby said, low-voiced. "Your mother's letter . . . after all this time . . . I could not bear to think of her so near . . . and then, I heard quite out of the blue about your brother . . . my grandson, in such danger . . . and I had not even known . . ."

"My dear ma'am, you must not distress yourself so. Do you have a smelling bottle?"

"No, no! I am not so . . . A moment and I shall recover myself."

"But you must allow me to send for something . . . a little brandy, perhaps . . ." A violent denial greeted this. "Some cordial then, or a dish of tea . . ."

"You are very kind, but I have no wish to trouble anyone."

"It won't be the least bit of trouble," Kate said with an encouraging smile. "As it happens, I have already asked Grayson to have a tea tray sent up."

"Well, in that case . . . tea would be very welcome."

By the time Kate's mother returned, Lady Welby had recovered her color a little. Even so, her daugh-

ter's joy upon seeing her brought the easy tears to
Lady Welby's eyes again, so that it was an emo-
tional reunion. Kate quietly left the room, and it
was doubtful if either woman noticed she had
gone.

"You must have wondered . . ." the old lady said
presently. "All those years of silence?"

"I was hurt—and very bitter at first," Lady Elizabeth admitted. "But after my umpteenth letter had
been ignored, I became resigned. Until, that is, we
arranged our present visit to London, when I decided to try one more time."

There was a curious pause. Then: "It is not easy
for me to . . . to say this, Elizabeth . . ." The frail
voice faltered; she drew breath. "The fact is, you
see, I never received your letters."

"But . . ."

"Please, hear me out, my dear. You must have
known that your father is . . . was never an easy
man, although he has many admirable qualities,
and that being the case, he could not or would not
condone or forgive what you had done. I was forbidden to get in touch, or in any way communicate." The old lady paused and drew a shuddering
breath. "I daresay I should have been stronger, but
you know how he could be. I was never very good
at standing up to him. And, once we had given up
the Town house and retired to Merton, I felt iso-
lated, and it was all too easy to lose contact with
such friends as we might have retained. What I did
not know until very recently, is that he ordered
James to burn your letters unopened the moment
they arrived . . ." She heard her daughter gasp.
"And to do the same with any I might write to
you."

"Mama! Oh, but that is monstrous! How could
he?" Lady Elizabeth cried.

"All too easily, it seems. It is only very recently,

since he . . . he suffered a severe seizure which has left him paralyzed . . ." again she heard her daughter catch her breath, ". . . that I discovered what had happened, for when your recent letter came, James, unsure what to do, brought it to me."

Their tears mingled as they mourned the lost years, and when Kate returned, she found them hand in hand, red-eyed, but well on the way to being reconciled.

"And now I have a grandmother. What fun," she said.

It was decided after much discussion that when Lady Welby felt strong enough, she would return home, and that Patrick would follow her to Merton to assess Lord Welby's condition, after which a nurse would be hired, so that Lady Welby could have a few days in Town with her daughter before they returned to Ireland.

Blaise did not attend Lady Chessington's ball. Kate told herself that it was no more than she had expected. And besides, she had no need of him, for every dance was spoken for within a few minutes of her arrival. Nor had she chosen her very becoming gown of amber silk embellished with little gold acorns in the hope that he might compliment her upon it. Indeed, there were many others only too eager to shower her with compliments, but, as in the case of Charlie Stanford, she found them all too gushing.

Mr. Merivale was there, however, and his compliments were more restrained, and gratefully accepted.

As if he sensed her disappointment, he casually endeavored to find excuses for his friend. "These past few years Blaise has schooled himself to care for nothing, d'ye see. Not that he don't love his children, mind. But like a hurt animal, he has been wary of trusting anything or anyone else. However, ... " his eyes twinkled, "I have seen a decided change in him of late."

"Well, I am very glad if that is so," she returned carelessly. "Not that it concerns me in the least."

"Quite so," he agreed equably. "Just thought I'd mention it."

# Seventeen

Almack's was everything Blaise had said of it. But for all that, Kate found it an interesting experience. The rooms were spacious and well lit, but unremarkable by comparison with many of the great houses she had visited.

Lady Jersey came forward to greet them, and to introduce the other Patronesses present to Kate. Countess Lieven, wife of the Russian ambassador, greeted her graciously enough, but had a decided air of hauteur. Lady Sefton and Lady Cowper, however, were delighted to see her and made her very welcome.

She was pleased to see that Chloe had already arrived with her mama, though she was looking a trifle pale and something less than her usual bubbly self.

"I had so hoped that Kit would be able to come with you this evening," she whispered to Kate. "But your father would not hear of his attempting it, and Mama would not hear of me staying at home to bear him company. Oh, Kate, I am quite wretched."

"Be patient," Kate said, though, much as she loved her brother, she could hold out no great hope of his wishing to be tied down. And even if he did, Lady Melchester, warm and kind as she was, must surely entertain much higher aspirations for her daughter than to see her married to a devil-may-care one-armed soldier with no fortune, even if he was fortunate enough to enjoy the Duke of Wellington's favor. And who could blame her, Kate thought, striving to be impartial.

"I quite thought that by now you would have tired of this eternal round of pleasure," Blaise murmured quizzically, coming upon her between dances.

"Then you would be quite mistaken," she murmured, "for it is endlessly diverting—like one of those children's games where you dance 'round and 'round in a ring under the watchful eyes of the governess"—she glanced across at the formidable countess—"until, sooner or later, you find yourself with the same partner. And exchange trivial politenesses."

His smile became a trifle cynical as he followed her gaze. "Do not let that particular governess hear you say so. Madame de Lieven, in common with the other *grandes dames*, has the power to banish you into the outer darkness forthwith—and not just from these assembly rooms."

"Oh, come now, Blaise! I have cut my eye teeth, you know."

"I don't doubt it, my dear girl. But you underestimate the power of these formidable ladies at your peril." He put up his eyeglass to glance across at the small group surrounding his mother. "I see Lazenby is here," he murmured dryly. "One meets him everywhere these days, or at least wherever Mama is likely to be present."

"I think he's sweet on her," Kate said, a smile dimpling her cheek. "And why not? Your mother is a lovely lady." She saw he was regarding her with something like awe. "And Sir Dominic has a great deal of address, you know, which is what, I suppose, makes him such an excellent diplomat."

"Very likely." His eyebrows drew together in a frown. "And when duty and pleasure combine, who knows what may transpire." Then, abruptly, he said, "Is this waltz spoken for, Kate, or may I claim it?"

She tried not to read into his wishing to dance with her anything more than a strong sense of duty to her as his mother's protégée, for that moment of intimacy in the Rose Saloon had never come close to being repeated. Yet as he whirled her around, she could not still that leap in her blood that made her achingly conscious of his hand, firm and warm through the thin *mousseline de soie* of her gown, his breath stirring her hair as his head bent close to hers, and she could only pray that the thudding of her heart would not betray her.

Once, as she was swirled around, Kate thought she glimpsed Amelia Broughton, but the dizzying lights were playing tricks with her eyes and she could not be sure.

From across the room, Lady St. Clair watched Kate and Blaise dancing, and, hardly daring to hope, said, "Kate looks particularly well this evening, don't you think, Dominic?"

He raised his glass to watch the young girl circling the floor with St. Clair. "Very fine," he agreed. "She is a charming child. Charming enough to captivate your son, do you suppose?"

"I could wish it so," the marchioness murmured with a sigh. "There have been moments recently when I have thought . . . but, no sooner do I hope than they are at odds again."

"Sounds promising." He chuckled at her look of mystification. "Lord, Alicia, there's more than one way to pursue a courtship. Which brings me to a matter very close to my heart." He grew suddenly serious. "I am being sent to Paris shortly—"

"But I thought you were to be here indefinitely!" She was astonished to discover how much she minded.

His elegant shoulders lifted in a wry shrug. "Wellington seems to believe that my considerable diplomatic experience will be of use in helping to calm troubled waters—bring opposing factions together."

"Well, it is very flattering that he should regard you so highly, and indeed, so he should . . ." Dear God, she was gabbling like an ingenue, "but . . ."

"And so I thought how very much more agreeable my task would be if I had a wife beside me to charm the intransigents into submission . . ."

"A wife!" Her heart was beating very fast. "But you have always avowed that you would never . . ."

"A wife who is beautiful and wise and remarkably clever at smoothing troubled waters . . . and has always made every other woman seem less than perfect by comparison," he swept on, encouraged by the rush of confusion that swept her face. "A woman I have loved at a distance for many years, and who is presently blushing quite delightfully."

Her ladyship's emotions were in turmoil, her eyes misted so that she did not see a middle-aged exquisite. Instead, he had become again that young and fascinating friend of Edward's, quick-witted and with charm enough to coax the birds from the trees—or, as he had done many times, no doubt, a pretty woman into his bed. He had wanted her then, she thought, but not once had he attempted to cuckold Edward. Oh, heavens, what a coil!

"Dominic! How could you spring this on me . . ." she protested, to give herself time to think, ". . . in this most public of places! I am sure that everyone will be looking . . ."

"I would gladly take you somewhere more private."

"Stop, oh, stop!" The beating of her heart had almost reached suffocation point. "I cannot—will not—be rushed! There are so many decisions . . . the children to be thought of . . . and Blaise . . ."

"Blaise is quite capable of thinking for himself, and for his children. You have nannied him far too long as it is. And I must tell you that time is short." Sir Dominic's eyes blazed down at her. "My dearest girl, this can hardly have come as a surprise. Any fool must have seen that I have been ogling you for weeks now."

"Dominic!" Girl! He had called her a girl. And though she affected to be shocked, her heart beat like that of any green girl, and her eyes betrayed her. "I refuse to have my intentions made known here," she cried, affecting indignation. "Come to dinner tomorrow evening, and you shall have your answer."

Charlie Stanford had arrived late, having been involved in a curricle race against an old adversary, which he had lost, leaving him bad-tempered and poorer by several hundred guineas. His temper was not improved by finding Kate so much in demand. The sight of her in Blaise's arms had done little to cheer him, for there was something about the way they danced—a kind of intimacy—that aroused the demon jealousy. St. Clair was everything that he wished to be, and had not as yet achieved—urban, top-lofty, a Corinthian of the first water. Until recently he had cheerfully accepted that time would remedy any shortcomings.

But that was before Kate Sheridan had come upon the scene. She was not like most young women of his acquaintance; she did not simper, or flutter her eyelashes, or make fun of his tendency

to blush as many of Chloe's friends did. In effect,
she made him feel much more a man of the world.
And this being so, he had begun to resent any other
man's paying her undue attentions.

"I have hardly seen you since Lady Chessington's ball," he said, unable to remove the note of
petulance from his voice upon finding himself beside her at last.

His face was a trifle flushed and Kate thought
she detected a faint whiff of brandy on his breath.

"I have been rather preoccupied with family
matters of late," she explained soothingly, wishing
to avert a scene.

"Of course, y'r brother," he said, annoyed with
himself for appearing unsympathetic. "Heard he
was well on the mend now, though."

"Thank you, yes." As the sets began to form for a
country dance, Kate saw Blaise on the far side of
the room, his head bent in a gesture of intimacy toward a face, quite beautiful in profile, uplifted to
him in a gesture almost of supplication, the shining
hair beautifully coiffured . . .

Charlie, seeing her fixed expression, followed the
direction of her glance. "Aha, Amelia Broughton. I
thought it wouldn't be long before she was back in
favor," he said, not even trying to keep the satisfaction out of his voice. "Time was when they were in-
separable, until St. Clair got cold feet. Amelia was
furious and took up with Tethington's heir, but that
came to nought. In any case, as I believe I once told
you, it was ever St. Clair she wanted, and Amelia
has a way of getting what she wants."

There was a momentary look of blind distress in
his companion's eyes that urged him to draw her
into a deserted corner where, unable to contain his
feelings any longer, he blurted out, "Oh, Kate,
d-dearest Kate . . . forget about St. Clair. He ain't
worthy of your love. Give me leave instead to ap-

proach your father . . . offer for your hand . . . have adored you from the first . . ."

Dismay at seeing Blaise and Amelia Broughton in such revealing closeness, followed by Charlie's sudden and quite unexpected declaration, made Kate blurt out unthinkingly, "Don't be silly, Charlie!" And then, seeing him reel as though she had struck him, "Oh, I am so sorry! Truly, I did not mean . . ."

"I know well enough what you meant," Charlie stuttered, red-faced and refusing to be mollified. He had laid his heart at her feet and she had cruelly crushed it. "I only hope you don't live to regret your decision," he added spitefully, turning blindly to leave her. "You may have received a deal of attention, but with no fortune to speak of, I doubt you will find offers of marriage that easy to come by."

His departure, and the bout of ill-temper that preceded it, caused something of a stir among those nearby, but Kate was too upset to notice their spiteful amusement. She would not have hurt Charlie for the world. She told Chloe so, having recounted the gist of what had happened without mentioning Blaise.

"Oh, I shouldn't worry about Charlie," Chloe said carelessly. "He will go off and shoot a few rabbits, and forget you in no time at all."

This, if not exactly flattering, relieved her mind a little. Mr. Merivale, having witnessed the little scene, came upon her shortly afterward to claim his dance.

"Word to the wise, m'dear girl," he murmured gently. "It don't do to go aside with a young man here." He saw the stormy expression in her eyes and added soothingly, "Just thought I'd mention it. The eagle-eyed Patronesses don't take kindly to anything resembling scandalous flirtation within these hallowed walls."

"Perhaps you should remind Blaise of that fact," Kate snapped, and was immediately mortified by her impetuosity, the more so as his gentle smile demonstrated his obvious concern for her, melting her anger. "I'm sorry, Gervase," she said ruefully, explaining briefly what had happened, skating briefly over Charlie's spiteful remarks upon seeing Blaise with Amelia Broughton and concentrating upon his precipitate proposal. "Charlie took me by surprise, you see. But you are quite right to reproach me. I handled the whole thing very badly. Poor Charlie. What a shrew he will think me."

"No one could ever think you that, m'dear," Mr. Merivale assured her, inwardly digesting what she had let fall concerning Blaise. He too had marked Amelia's presence with some apprehension, but that Kate should be aware of it, and should react so vehemently, both interested and disturbed him.

As they took their places for the dance, he murmured obliquely, "It don't do to read too much into what you see, m'dear. Things are not always what they seem."

His words left Kate to wonder just how much he knew. But her evening was spoiled, and she could not wait for it to end. The incident with Charlie seemed to have passed without comment, except for a moment near the end. As Lady Cowper was leaving she tapped her with her fan in passing, and said in gentle reproof, "Do have a care, my dear. Decorum is everything in a young girl."

"You seem a little down-pin, Kate," observed Lady St. Clair the following morning, observing her godchild's rather hollow-eyed look.

"I woke early and couldn't get back to sleep again," Kate said swiftly.

"Ah, well," murmured the marchioness, who, on

the contrary, seemed in remarkably good spirits, "I expect the worry of the past few weeks is catching up with you."

"I expect that is it."

"I hope you will feel better by this evening. I thought a quiet little impromptu dinner party would be pleasant. Just family, you know—yours and mine, and a few close friends, before your parents prepare to go home. I begin to agree with Blaise that a surfeit of balls can wear one down."

Kate wondered if she could feign a migraine, or some other minor disability—anything that would prevent her from having to meet Blaise, trying to behave as though nothing had happened. Except, of course, that as far as he was aware, nothing had. And if she cried off, Mama would worry and her father was much too acute not to know that she was feigning illness.

She decided that fresh air was what she needed, and offered to take the children to Hyde Park once their lessons were at an end, to give Miss Glynn a break. At the last minute Kit arrived and offered to accompany them, much to Freddie's delight. He was walking quite well now with just the aid of a stick.

The sun was shining and they stayed for a while by the Serpentine.

"Grandmama said they had a pretend naval battle here last year," Freddie said wistfully. "I wish I could have seen it."

"Well, we could have a battle of our own," said Kit, and showed Freddie how to make little boats out of leaves with tiny twigs for sails. He was becoming remarkably deft at managing with one arm.

He and Freddie spent some time sinking one another's boats, and Freddie got his breeches wet.

"Miss Glynn'll be cross," he said happily.

Kit laughed. "You don't sound particularly

scared, my boy. Clearly, you are destined to be a military man of some kind."

"Kit, don't encourage him," Kate said, mindful of Blaise's recent comments.

"Oh, well," Freddie sighed, and then brightened. "Oh see, Kate, there's Joss! Can I go and talk to him?"

She hesitated. "Very well. But only for a moment. I suspect he shouldn't really be here at all."

Ellen had returned to Mount Street, her mother now being fully recovered from the stomach pains that had struck her down. She had been full of how well Joss had fitted into the family, and how her father thought Joss had a definite way with horses.

Kate, watching the two boys, heads together as they examined the make-believe boats and discussed battle tactics, thought how like them Kit had been as a boy. Still was, deep down—a small boy fighting battles. Her smile faded as she glanced at the empty sleeve. Except, that now, the enemy was real—and fought back.

"Joss said there are some jugglers performing in a park near where he lives a week from now," Freddie said, as Joss finally ran off and he came trotting back. "I suppose I couldn't . . . ?"

"No, you couldn't," she replied, well aware of how his father would react to the merest suggestion. And when his lip quivered mutinously and he looked set to argue, she said sharply, "Freddie, do stop being tiresome about it. You know your father's views about Joss. And besides, you are much too young to be out at night."

"Well, it's not fair," he muttered, kicking at the grass. "Joss isn't much older than me."

Kate looked beseechingly at Kit, who said, quite sternly for him, "Now, listen to me, young shaver. If we're talking about fair—life frequently isn't fair, so everyone has to learn discipline, and the earlier, the better. I thought my father was fearsome strict with me when I was your age, but I was glad of it later, for army discipline is even more fearsome, believe me—and I doubt I would have stuck it out without that early training."

Kate was surprised and grateful to him, and although Freddie still sulked for a while, and wouldn't quite meet her eyes, he was soon skipping beside Kit, who beguiled him back into a good humor once more.

# *Eighteen*

They sat down twelve to dinner that evening. The number included Kate's parents and Kit, the Melchesters and Chloe, Sir Dominic, and Mr. Merivale. Miss Priddy had to be persuaded, saying she would far rather sit with Lady Welby, who had now arrived to stay for a few days in Mount Street but was not up to company.

"Do I get the impression that this is no ordinary occasion?" murmured Mr. Merivale, threading his way through the little groups gathered in the drawing room beforehand to rescue Blaise from the nervously vociferous Miss Priddy, who, finding herself alone with the marquess, had launched into a somewhat incoherent account of the latest doings of her friend, Miss Payne.

"Lord, don't ask me, Gervase," Blaise said, his glass raised to watch his mother in animated conversation with the Melchesters and Lazenby. She looked particularly fine this evening, he thought, in her favorite silver-gray with her hair dressed around a pretty lace cap. There was, it seemed, a particular kind of glow about her. "True, it's not like her to arrange dinner parties in such a skimble-scamble, spur-of-the-moment way . . ."

Irresistibly, he allowed his gaze to move on to Kate, who was standing with her parents, and who, by contrast, in spite of her shining hair and ravishing blush-pink gown, seemed a trifle listless. He turned back to Gervase.

"It may of course have something to do with the fact that Sir Dominic is to leave shortly for Paris. As this seems to be one of the few nights when no one of note is holding a ball or somesuch, Mama possibly thought to give him a grand send-off."

"Sounds reasonable."

"It does, doesn't it?" Blaise agreed.

"Been seeing a lot of Lazenby recently, of course," Mr. Merivale observed obliquely. "Daresay she'll miss him."

"Quite probably."

It was quite unlike Kate to feel so out of sorts. Her walk with Kit earlier had cheered her up considerably. But now all his attention was reserved for Chloe, and she was hanging on his every word until they all went in to dinner, when they were separated and reduced to exchanging speaking glances across the table, leading Kate to conclude, with unaccustomed cynicism, that being in love was a most antisocial preoccupation, and one in which she resolved never to embroil herself.

However, since she was seated between her godmother and Lord Melchester, an entertaining but verbose gentleman, and since the marchioness had Sir Dominic on her other side, the table talk was sufficiently enlivening and informal for no one to notice how little Kate herself contributed. She might even be able to slip away later, pleading a headache, without attracting too much comment.

But when that time came, all thought of doing so was banished, for Sir Dominic stood up and tapped his glass for silence.

"I make no apology for interrupting your no-doubt erudite conversations," he began, "for we are all good friends, and friends may occasionally take liberties with convention."

There was some laughter.

"I shall not keep you long," he continued, his rich voice grown fruitier with the aid of an excellent burgundy, "but this is, as you may have guessed, no ordinary occasion. When I arrived home from Brazil, I thought I was home for good—an honorable retirement from active service in which to rest my weary bones and drift pleasantly into the sunset of my years . . ."

There was another ripple of laughter and Lord Melchester exclaimed, "You drift? Not a chance, old lad . . ."

Sir Dominic lifted his glass and took a drink. "Instead, I am commanded to leave shortly for Paris, to act, as far as I am able, as a mediator between disaffected factions . . ."

"No better man for the job," someone said, and Kate thought so, too, though her godmother would miss him. Not that she seemed in the least distressed at present. If anything, she was looking rather pink and embarrassed.

". . . but this time I shall not be going alone." Sir Dominic's eyes were very bright as they swept the table. "For Alicia, who is dear to you all, and has been more than dear to me for many years, has consented to come with me as my wife."

There was a moment of absolute silence, followed by pandemonium as congratulations came from all sides, Kate being one of the first to hug her and whisper her joy. And above all the hubbub, Miss Priddy's voice tremulously upraised: "Oh, my dear Lady St. Clair! Such a wonderful surprise . . . so romantic . . ."

Amid the confusion, Blaise quietly rose from his seat and made his way to his mother's side, where he folded her in his arms, and Kate heard him say quietly, "About time, too, dearest Ma. I couldn't be more pleased."

"Oh, my dear boy! I was so afraid . . . I should have told you, but everything happened so quickly . . ."

"So it would seem." Blaise looked up at Sir Dominic, a gleam in his eyes. "I had a feeling something was going on. As head of the family, I could, of course, withhold my consent . . ."

Sir Dominic grinned broadly back at him. "A fig for your consent, my boy. I'm too old to be called out, and I've been in love with y'r mother far too long to give her up now."

"Then I can only wish you both very happy," he said, shaking Sir Dominic warmly by the hand. His eyes lifted to rest upon his mother, who was laughing and blushing like a young girl. "These past few weeks have made me realize how selfishly I have depended upon Mama. It is high time she thought of herself and took up her own life again."

Kate felt the tears pricking her eyes as she stood with her parents watching the happy scene. "I don't think I have ever seen anyone so filled with joy."

"A very happy outcome," said Mr. Merivale, coming to join them. "And not all that unexpected."

"You guessed!" Kate exclaimed.

"The merest suspicion," he said modestly.

"I remember when we were all young," her mother recalled, misty-eyed. "Sir Dominic was in love with her then, you know. But although she was fond of him, she had eyes only for Edward. And to think that across all the years his feelings have not changed!"

"I think it is the most romantic story I ever heard," said Kate.

"Not that Dominic won't have led a full and eventful life since then," her father added dryly, coming to join them. "He was a great charmer as a young man, and, fine man and excellent diplomat though he is, I doubt he has been celibate for many of those years."

"Patrick!" Lady Elizabeth was scandalized. "How could you? And in front of your own daughter!"

"Ah, sure, Kate knows what's what, don't you, my love?"

She laughed. "Well enough, Pa. Will you look at poor Chloe? And her wishing it was herself and Kit."

"Young love! The pain of it. But, there's time enough for them."

That evening was the start of a hectic two weeks. Sir Dominic had told his bride-to-be not to concern herself with a trousseau, for there were excellent modistes a'plenty in Paris. They were to be married quietly in a nearby church in a little over a week's time, and would sail for France two days later.

It was difficult to discern how the children felt about their grandmama's imminent departure. She was, in Roseanne's case, at least, the nearest thing to a mother they had ever known. Freddie affected not to care, which fooled no one. But Roseanne grew very quiet and withdrawn.

"I shan't be all that far away, my darlings," she had promised them, fighting back her tears. "And the time will pass very quickly. I daresay I shall be back to see you almost before you have had time to miss me, for Sir Dominic will be required to visit to London quite often, you know, and naturally I shall come to visit you at Kimberley."

"But it won't be the same," Freddie muttered sullenly.

"No. But then life is full of change. That is what makes it so exciting—that we never quite know what is going to happen next. Like you and

Roseanne returning to Grosvenor Square tomorrow to be with your father." He seemed less than pleased, so she added quickly, "And only think, you will be going back to Kimberley very soon, and Cherry will be waiting for you. I expect he is missing you."

His face brightened very slightly at this thought. And then he heaved an enormous sigh as Kate came into the room. "I 'spect you will be leaving soon as well. Then there'll only be Miss Glynn."

"And your father," said Lady St. Clair. "I hope you mean to be a good boy and make him proud of you."

"I suppose so. But I don't see why you want to marry Sir Dominic when you have Papa," he persisted, convinced that weddings were only for simpering girls.

"I love your father very much, Freddie dear," she tried to explain to him, "but it is a different kind of love, as you will understand when you are older. He is my son, just as you are his son."

This didn't wholly satisfy Freddie, but he said that he supposed when you were grown up you could do as you liked. His face brightened as he thought about this.

"When I'm grown up," he said, "I mean to be a soldier like Kit."

Kate and the marchioness exchanged glances, but it seemed wiser not to upset him further by demolishing any more of his cherished notions.

"He'll soon get over it," Kate said when he remained quieter than normal.

Miss Priddy had been Lady St. Clair's other great worry, over whom she had agonized long and hard. Dear Priddy, who had been so grateful for so little, even if she did occasionally drive one to distraction.

"You surely don't mean to take her to Paris," Sir

Dominic had exclaimed, horrified. "For I warn you, it won't do!"

His beloved's trill of laughter only partially reassured him.

"I hope I know you better than to suggest it. But I do feel responsible for her."

"Then pension her off, my love."

"But she has nowhere to go—no relations that I know of . . ."

"Then we'll find her a cottage—near Kimberley, perhaps. Blaise's agent would know of somewhere, I'm sure."

It had seemed very straightforward when Dominic suggested it, but looking into that eager innocent face, the marchioness felt like a traitor. But, in the end, it had been easy.

"You must not think that I mean to abandon you, Priddy," she had begun.

"Oh, no, indeed! As if you would, dear Lady St. Clair!" she had exclaimed, clutching her shawl about her. "It is the most extraordinary thing, for Miss Amelia Payne—you may remember the friend I told you about—well, it is no more than a day or two since, she asked me if I would consider coming to share her little house . . . and I have been trying to find a way to broach the subject . . . It is almost as if it were meant, don't you think?"

Lady St. Clair scarcely knew whether to laugh or cry with relief. "Well, if that is what you would like . . . ?"

"Indeed, yes, above all things! Oh, not that I have not been happy . . . such kindness . . ." Miss Priddy's cheeks grew pink. "But I am no longer young, and as Amelia says, two can live almost as cheaply as one, and I have a little money saved."

"Even so, I shall insist on providing you with a pension—say, thirty guineas a year?"

Miss Priddy grew even pinker. "So kind . . . so good . . ."

And so all was most amicably settled, and almost before they knew it, the wedding day arrived. It was just as the couple had wished. News of their betrothal could not be kept quiet for long, and there had been much rejoicing, but the time and date of the wedding had been kept a close secret. Their greatest fear had been that news of it would spread, turning the whole affair into a circus, but the secret held and only family and the closest friends were present to see Lady St. Clair become Lady Lazenby. She looked delightful in oyster silk with a matching stylish bonnet trimmed with pale pink ribbons, and she carried pink roses.

Kate had resolved to be sensible, but she was obliged to swallow a lump in her throat when Blaise entered the church with his mother on his arm. There was something so infinitely moving about the closeness of mother and son in that moment, and she prayed that no one would see her wipe away a tear.

It was a short service, and was followed by a reception at the house in Grosvenor Square, enjoyed by all amid much laughter and tears.

"Don't care much for bridals, as a rule," murmured Mr. Merivale, "but it has all gone rather well, don't y' think?"

"Yes, indeed," Kate agreed, feeling suddenly, unaccountably flat. "Exactly as her ladyship wished it to be."

He put up his glass. "You look a little like a bride yourself, m'dear, in that pretty white muslin. Most charming."

"It was not my intention," she said abruptly. Then, every inch aware of how perceptive he could be, she added lightly, "I just thought—you know—something simple."

"Would that others had followed your example," he said, watching Lady Melchester sway across the room under the weight of an enormous, overembellished bonnet.

Kate stifled a laugh. "It is rather extreme, is it not? But she is so nice, one cannot be unkind about it."

"Perhaps not, but it does not bode well for the day when it is Chloe's turn to walk up the aisle. How goes that little affair? Do you know?"

Kate confessed that she did not know. "I'm not sure that Kit would make a good husband, dearly though I love him. And if he is to join the Duke's staff, he could be traveling a great deal." She sighed. "Perhaps it is no more than a romantic attachment."

"Perhaps," he agreed.

Sir Dominic and his glowing bride left Grosvenor Square late in the day in a carriage piled high with portmanteaux and bandboxes, bound for an unknown destination, before setting sail for France.

"Kate, my dear," she confessed between tears and joy, as the carriage waited at the door, "I cannot help feeling that I am letting you down—to be abandoning you in this ramshackle way before your stay with me is at an end . . ."

"But you are not, dearest of godmothers! You have given me the most splendid time, and I wouldn't have missed it for the world! It gives me so much pleasure now to see you so happy . . ."

"Even so, to be flinging my bonnet over the windmill in such a ridiculous fashion, like any green girl! I cannot think how I let Dominic talk me into it!"

"I am very glad he did."

"Well, at least it is almost certain that your mother will stay on for a while at Mount Street, in order to try and resolve matters with your grandparents."

"Yes. Pa has certain commitments in Dublin, so he may have to go home and come back again . . ."

"Alicia, my love! The horses are growing restive . . ." Sir Dominic, larger than life, strode into the room, filling it with his ebullient personality.

She blushed like any bride half her age, and then they were gone in a flurry of good-byes, while the children, caught up in the atmosphere, waved as excitedly as the rest.

Only when the carriage had disappeared from view did Freddie suddenly turn and run inside.

"Let him be for a while," Lady Elizabeth said quietly. "He'll soon come around."

The wedding of Sir Dominic and Lady St. Clair was the talk of every social gathering for the next few days, until something more scandalous came along to take its place.

"So sly of them to deprive us of the pleasure of seeing them married," Lady Jersey said playfully, meeting Kate and her mother several evenings later. "Even so, one wishes them very happy, I'm sure. They will be on their way to Paris by now, I daresay."

"Possibly," agreed Lady Elizabeth. "Sir Dominic was all secrecy when they left, but he did send word to say they would be crossing to France yesterday."

# Nineteen

Kate, with her parents and Kit, was enjoying a quiet dinner when there was a sound of hurried footsteps and the marquess burst in upon them, coattails flying, his deep-set blue eyes vivid beneath the black brows. Such a breach of good manners was so foreign to him that Kate was alarmed.

"Blaise! What . . . ?" She half-rose from her chair, her first thought being that something had happened to his mother.

"Forgive me. A matter of urgency . . . Grayson admitted me and I said I would see myself up. I have to know—is Freddie here?"

Dr. Sheridan also rose to his feet, laying aside his napkin. The very calmness of the gesture seemed to have an effect.

"No, he is not. Why? Should he be?"

"He should be in his bed." The words were ground out. "Miss Glynn banished him there this afternoon after he had been rebellious and disobedient, but when she looked in an hour or so later, he was not there."

"It is not unusual for small boys to play tricks, especially when the usual pattern of their lives has been upset, for whatever reason."

"I excelled at it," Kit put in, and earned himself a reproachful look from his mother. But his lordship seemed not to have heard.

"We have searched every inch of the house," he said, his voice betraying an underlying fear, "and he is not to be found."

"Oh, poor Freddie," Kate exclaimed, pushing back her chair as she saw how tautly his face was set. "Your mother's going upset him quite badly, I think."

"Would you like us to come around?" Lady Elizabeth suggested.

"I think not. There is always the chance that he might come here. The servants are out at present searching the surrounding area . . . and Miss Glynn is having hysterics." There was a haunted look in his eyes. "Freddie is only six."

"But very sensible for his age," Lady Elizabeth said quietly.

"Perhaps. But he has been in a very rebellious mood of late."

"Many things around him are changing," Dr. Sheridan said quietly. "It can be very unsettling for children, especially intelligent children like Freddie."

The marquess groaned. "I should have taken them back to Kimberley as soon as Freddie had seen the dentist." He hesitated, as if realizing for the first time that he was disturbing their dinner. "I'm sorry—I shouldn't have . . ."

"No matter," said Dr. Sheridan. "We had all but finished anyway."

"Kit and I shall come around at any rate," Kate insisted. "He can't have gone far."

"You think not?" he said with a harshness that made her heart turn over. "Then let me tell you, my dear Kate, there are evil men in this town on the lookout for boys like Freddie."

"You are jumping to conclusions, Blaise," Dr. Sheridan said quietly.

"I wonder . . ." Kit began, then hesitated, cocking

an eyebrow. "Jugglers?" he suggested, looking at Kate as all eyes turned on them.

She suddenly remembered how Freddie had refused to meet her eyes that afternoon in the park. Suppose he and Joss had arranged it then? "You could be right. But where? Ellen would probably know . . ." Trying not to hope, she ran to the door.

"One moment." It was Blaise, coldly commanding, and she turned to face him. The black bar of his brows quivered menacingly. "What exactly might Ellen know?"

She could not look away from his dagger-sharp eyes.

It was Kit who said calmly, "There was a lad in the Park the other day—black curly hair—knew Freddie. He was telling him some tale about jugglers on the green near his home . . ."

"Joss." Blaise ground the name out as his gaze swung back to Kate.

"Aye. That was his name," Kit agreed.

"You allowed my son to talk to that ragamuffin?"

"It wasn't a case of allowing," Kate returned, anger and guilt evident in her stormy eyes. "They had already met—and anyway, there was no question of Freddie being allowed to see the jugglers. Kit spoke very sternly to him . . ."

"I am obliged," said Blaise through gritted teeth.

"No sayin' he'd take notice, of course," Kit added.

"Plainly he did not. So, the fact remains that my son might now be in some squalid little back street—*if he ever got that far*—mixing with God knows what riff and raff—"

"Then the sooner Ellen is consulted, the sooner we may find him," said Dr. Sheridan, calmly commanding. "All recriminations can surely wait until the boy is safe."

"Yes, of course. You are right."

After that, everything seemed to happen very quickly. Ellen, when told, was horrified. "Joss'll get a leatherin' for this—eggin' on 'is young lordship an' leading 'im astray."

"Oh, for heaven's sake, Ellen, don't let's start apportioning blame! If you'll just tell us where to go."

"I'd best come with you, Miss Kate. I'm no good at givin' directions . . ."

The carriage was summoned, and with a tight-lipped Pogson on the box, Kate, with a scared and silent Ellen beside her, together with Dr. Sheridan and the marquess, made all speed to the area of Shoreditch where Ellen's family lived, while Lady Elizabeth stayed in Mount Street, and Kit went to Grosvenor Square in case the boy should arrive home in their absence.

The sounds of laughter and cheering, and the flickering of torch flames reached them while the carriage was still some way off. Kate, praying as she had never prayed before, could hardly wait for the vehicle to stop on the corner of the street.

"Wait here," Blaise said abruptly, opening the door.

"I will not," she retorted, ignoring the look he shot back at her. "The more of us who look, the quicker we'll find him. Ellen, you go with my father, and I'll stay with the marquess."

"Go careful—an' watch out fer pickpockets," Ellen muttered, embarrassed.

Neither of them spoke as they pushed their way through the jostling crowd, Kate ignoring the whistles and bawdy invitations as they sought to avoid contact with sweat-soaked bodies.

A place seemed to have been made near the front for the younger children, and it was here, when Kate was close to despair, that she caught a glimpse of Freddie, laughing and jumping up and down with those around him. She laid a hand on Blaise's arm and pointed him out.

"Let me go," she pleaded, as he made to lunge forward. "We don't want to frighten him, or cause any trouble among the crowd."

Blaise looked furious and for a moment Kate thought he would not heed her. Then he said tersely, "Very well. But, for God's sake, be careful."

She eased her way through the remaining press of people, getting her bonnet knocked sideways as she avoided leering offers to "give yer a 'elpin' 'and, gel."

"My little boy," she murmured, her voice quivering with a panic that wasn't entirely false. "I have to get to him . . ."

"Gerr out the way . . . let the lassie past . . ." Kind voices egged her on, hands making a path for her, until she reached Freddie's side.

He was entirely wrapped up in a complex maneuver which involved six men climbing on one another's shoulders. He was shouting encouragement with the rest. His "Hurrah!" as the feat was accomplished ended in a gasp as Kate seized his arm.

"Oh knickerbockers!" he squeaked. "How did you . . . ?"

"Never mind how, my lad. Just thank your lucky stars it is me and not your father," she muttered, and looked across at Joss, who had torn his glance away from the spectacle and was eyeing her with some apprehension. "And you have a lot to answer for, Joss," she added.

"It weren't my fault, missus," he complained. "The young sprig wouldn't take no fer answer. I never thought as 'e'd go through wiv it, but I 'ad ter be where 'e said, for fear 'e'd try ter go by hisself. An' there 'e was, large as life." Joss sniffled. "I took care of 'im as best I could."

"Well, that at least is to your credit," she said, feeling a little sorry for him. "But you'll hear more of this, no doubt, when his lordship has time to deal with you."

Having said which, she dragged a yelping Freddie unceremoniously by his collar and a firmly held arm, back through the crowd, causing some mirth and much commiseration.

They arrived back at the coach to find that her father and Ellen had already returned, having failed to locate the boys. The marquess surveyed his disheveled and now apprehensive son in grim silence, and motioned him into the coach, still holding onto Kate's hand for what comfort could be derived. As his father was about to follow, Dr. Sheridan laid a hand on his arm.

"A word, Blaise," he said quietly. "May I suggest that you don't do anything in haste that you might later regret."

"He must be punished," said the marquess inflexibly.

"Agreed. He has put everyone to a great deal of trouble and worry. But punishment and love must go together. His life is at a crucial stage, and how you deal with him now may affect his whole future."

It was almost a lecture, something Blaise was not minded to endure lightly. Then he saw the outline of his son's face in the dimness of the carriage, its tautness noticeable even in the bad light as he leaned close to Kate. And he remembered how nearly, had circumstances been otherwise, he might have lost him.

"I am not a monster, sir," he said distantly.

Dr. Sheridan half-smiled. "I had not thought you were, m'boy. But, having reared three strong-willed sons of my own . . ."

"Quite."

*    *    *

Kate walked around to Grosvenor Square the following morning with her brother to inquire after Freddie.

The children were at their lessons, Jameson told them with a glint of sympathy in his eyes, and Miss Glynn did not wish them to be disturbed. It hadn't been too hard for Jameson to put two and two together following the upheavals of the previous evening, what with his lordship wearing his most unapproachable face this morning, and the little lad, so he had been told, looking very sorry for himself and sitting down very cautiously.

"I'll come back later then, if I may," Kate said.

"As to that, Miss Sheridan," Jameson said, straight-faced, "it is his lordship's intention to take the children back to Kimberley as soon as lessons are at an end. I believe he is at this moment engaged in making the arrangements."

"I see." Kate glanced at Kit, who shrugged his shoulders. She forced a smile for the butler's benefit. "Thank you, Jameson," and as she turned to go, added, "If the opportunity arises, will you tell them that I called and that I wish them well."

His eyes were sympathetic as he murmured his assent.

"That's the end of Freddie's visit to London, then," Kit said wryly as they returned home. "Poor little shaver, having Blaise for a father."

"Blaise is a very good father, as it happens," she protested, a little too vehemently, he thought. "He may find it difficult to show affection, but that doesn't mean he doesn't care!"

"True enough. Sorry if I spoke out of turn." He shot her a wry glance, and wisely refrained from further comment. "Did I tell you I'm to go for a medical examination in a couple of day's time?"

"No." Shaken out of her preoccupation, she

turned impulsively to him. "Surely you cannot yet be considered fit to return to active duties."

He grinned. "If you mean anything of an arduous nature, I think not. But I can manage light duties, and Wellington did promise me a staff appointment, if you remember."

"And you can't wait to get back among your fellow officers."

"Well, I can't say it hasn't been agreeable, being fussed over, once the worst was past, but time is beginning to hang a trifle heavy."

"And Chloe?" she asked.

"Ah, Chloe . . ." He looked for a moment like one of his younger brothers. "Yes, that might be a little difficult."

"Kit!" She stood still and faced him. "You cannot mean to drop poor Chloe, just like that, now you don't need her any more?"

"Put like that, it don't sound very chivalrous of me."

"No, it doesn't."

"I'm jolly fond of Chloe," he defended himself.

"And she is rather more than *jolly fond* of you, my lad."

"But you have to admit, she is still a little . . . immature." His grin was shamefaced. "Anyway, I ain't sure I'm ready to settle down yet, so I'd be doing her a favor, really."

"You're a beast, Kit Sheridan. And if I didn't agree with your last comment, I would cheerfully throttle you." Kate sighed, and added pleadingly, "Poor Chloe. You will let her down lightly, Kit?"

"Of course I will. Trust me."

It would be for the best; Kate knew that in her heart. She wondered how many girls he had loved and left so lightly. Men, she thought furiously—with a few exceptions, like her father, who would put up with them if they didn't have to?

She hadn't expected to see Blaise before he left, but to her surprise, his curricle was at the door with Pogson in charge as she and Kit returned to Mount Street. Pogson tipped his hat to them, and would have spoken, but at that moment the door opened to allow Grayson to show his lordship out.

"Ah, Kate. And Kit, too. I'm glad I have seen you." He sounded very formal.

"Young shaver none the worse for his adventure?" Kit asked cheerily.

A slight frown descended. "No. Just a little sadder and wiser, I trust."

Kit grinned. "He'll get over it."

"So I hope. I came around to thank you all for your help last evening. Though I cannot help feeling that it would never have happened but for . . ." He paused, looked briefly at Kate, and away again. "However, that is neither here nor there, now. I daresay Jameson will have told you we are leaving?"

"Taking the children back to Kimberley? Yes. I expect it is for the best."

"You are welcome to continue riding Mayfly whenever you wish, Kate. One of the grooms will accompany you."

"Thank you." How formal he was. And how unfair. She thought she could not bear it. Head high, she said, "I should like to see the children before they leave."

"I don't think that would be a good idea," he replied austerely. "Better not to unsettle them before the journey."

Insufferable! To her horror, she found that held-back tears were forming a lump at the back of her throat. But pride came to her aid. "You are quite right, of course. Much better. Then I wish you a safe journey," she managed before rushing indoors, leaving Kit to make her excuses.

By the time she went out that evening with the family to a small social gathering arranged by Lady Cowper, she was in a defiant mood. It was very obvious when she met Mr. Merivale and explained Blaise's absence.

"Come to cuffs, did you?"

"Oh, nothing so uncivilized," she retorted, and then, seeing his eyebrow lift fractionally, "Pay no heed to me, Gervase. I should not have come. I am blue-deviled and not fit to be in company."

"Which is hardly to be wondered at. The heat is becoming quite tiring," he said diplomatically, as if to excuse her. "And so is the Season. I have been wondering whether to retire to Brighton for a while—the sea breezes, y'know."

"Don't humor me, Gervase," she said abruptly. And then, contritely, "Oh, I am sorry! I seem always to be taking out my frustrations on you."

"I would say you are being remarkably restrained in the circumstances," he said, somewhat enigmatically. And then, quietly, "It is Blaise, of course."

"He is insufferable!"

"Oh, quite. But worthy of redemption, wouldn't you say?"

"If so, I am not the one to save him. He clearly means to cut me out of his life." Kate looked up at him. "Am I so transparent?"

"Only to me. I am fond of you both and if you can't save him, then no one can."

"There was a time when I . . ." Kate hesitated, then concluded defiantly, "But clearly I was wrong."

"Then I am sorry for you both," he said, and changed the subject. "Have you heard from Lady Lazenby?"

Kate pulled herself together and said brightly, "A brief letter only. She is obviously extremely happy and loving Paris. I could not be more pleased for

her. I daresay Blaise has more detailed news, but as
he is not here . . ."

Mr. Merivale wondered if she knew how much
her offhand manner betrayed her. What a fool
Blaise was. It was an accusation he had never
thought to lay at his friend's door, but fool he undoubtedly was, if not a coward—in love with Kate,
and afraid to admit the fact. What's more, he
would tell him so when next they met.

"And how do things stand with regard to your
grandparents?" he asked, deftly turning the conversation to safer territory.

"Better, I believe. Pa has persuaded Grandmama
to change their doctor, and has also secured the ser-
vices of an excellent, sensible nurse. He has also
arranged with Lord Welby's lawyer that unless and
until there is some marked improvement in Grand-
papa's condition, which seems unlikely, all matters
of business are to be dealt with jointly by himself
and my grandmother."

"That won't be easy for him, but I'm sure it will
be a great relief to Lady Welby. What a time you
have had, to be sure. One cannot say that your stay
here has lacked incident."

"No."

It was a small woeful sound, and he lightly
turned the subject. "Chloe Melchester is looking a
shade wan. Too many late nights beginning to tell,
do you think?"

"More likely, my fickle brother has conveyed to
her the news that he is about to leave us to resume
light duties with his regiment, and has done so
without declaring his intentions."

"She will get over him."

"Oh, undoubtedly. A soldier injured in a battle
must, I suppose, by the very nature of things, cut a
romantic figure. But I suspect that her parents will
be quietly relieved, for Kit, charming though he is,

has little else to commend him as a prospective husband."

"And charm don't pay the bills," Mr. Merivale acknowledged with a wry smile. "As I know to my cost."

"Quite." After a moment's silence, Kate said casually, "I have decided to go home with Ma and Pa when they leave on Friday."

He took a pinch of snuff. "We shall be very sorry to lose you," he said quietly. "You have brought a welcome breath of fresh air to this hot-house of insincerity and intrigue." *And Blaise is a fool if he cannot see it,* he added silently.

"Oh, but that is not true of everyone. I have enjoyed myself immensely and made many friends, whom I shall miss—you, most of all." *Except for one person,* she added silently. *And he is now beyond my reach. Perhaps he always was.*

"My dear Kate," Mr. Merivale murmured, clearly moved. "You are kinder than I deserve."

"No, I'm not. It is no less than the truth. But the Season will soon be at an end, you see, and I always find the final moment when a party ends terribly sad." She swallowed hard. "So, I have decided to slip away before this one does. Besides, it seems sensible to avail myself of the chance to travel with my parents."

# Twenty

Blaise hesitated at the gate of the gracious square house standing amid a pleasantly disordered array of flowers and greenery, listening to the sound of the retreating hack he had picked up on the quay. There was no turning back now, he thought, as the clip-clop of the hooves and the rattle of the wheels faded away. And his heart hollowed, for there were no certainties in what he was about to do.

He pushed open the gate, noticing as he did so the shining brass plate on the post proclaiming it to be the residence of Dr. Patrick Sheridan.

A pleasant-faced elderly maid dipped him a formal little curtsy, bade him a smiling, "You are welcome to this house," and ushered him through a cool slate-floored hall with a scattering of rugs, to a room at the rear, where she tapped and put her head around the door.

"Your visitor has arrived, doctor. Will I be showing him in?"

"Thank you, Mavis. If you will be so kind."

As the marquess entered, Dr. Sheridan laid aside the notes he was reading and came from behind a large mahogany desk to greet him.

"Blaise, I am delighted to see you. Do come and sit down. Will you take a glass of sherry?"

"Thank you, yes." The marquess settled himself in a leather armchair near the fireplace.

"Did you have a good crossing?"

"Tolerable." Blaise took the glass offered to him, and, looking up at the doctor, said without preamble, "How is Kate? Will she see me?"

Dr. Sheridan settled himself in a nearby chair, and regarded him thoughtfully. "To be perfectly honest, Blaise, I have not told Kate you were coming. She . . ." He chose his words carefully. "She has been very quiet since we came home. Not herself at all. She always rode a lot, but now she'll be off for hours alone." He sighed. "And, unhappy as she undoubtedly is, I had no wish to raise any false hopes."

The black brows drew together. "You believe I am responsible for that unhappiness?"

"I have not questioned her, not wanting to add to her distress, but I think we both know the answer to your question."

"Sir, I have been a great fool," Blaise admitted, staring down into the golden depths of his sherry. "And I have no excuses, except that I took Lucinda's death so badly that I vowed never to commit myself again . . ." He glanced up. "So that, when I knew I was falling in love with Kate, I fought against it with every fiber of my being. Took the coward's way, in fact." His voice was bitter. "Even though I knew that she was mine for the asking. And not a day has passed when I have not regretted my stupidity."

Dr. Sheridan regarded the bent head with compassion. "The heart is an unfathomable organ, my boy, for it is more than flesh and blood—and only time will heal its hurts and make it ready to love again." He looked searchingly at his young companion. "The question is, have you now reached that happy state?"

Kate came back from her ride to find her mother in the kitchen with Mavis. They stopped speaking as she came in, and Mavis blushed and became very busy. Kate pulled off her hat and her hair, carelessly pinned, fell down about her face. She pushed it back with impatient fingers.

"If you were talking about me, you may carry on," she said carelessly. "For I'm going up to wash and change. That sun is powerfully hot."

"Well, Miss Kate, if you will wear that old tweed habit when you've a fine new one hanging in your cupboard making a meal for the moths . . ."

Lady Elizabeth shot Mavis a warning glance which she did not heed.

"And you'll need to be making yourself dacent, for hasn't your father got a fine young titled gentleman closeted with him this half-hour past . . ."

"I can't see what father's patients have to do with me . . ." Kate's voice trailed away as she caught sight of her mother's face. "It isn't . . . ?" she whispered. "It can't be!" Panic rose in her. "Why is he here? Something has happened to the children!"

Lady Elizabeth watched the bright color fill her daughter's face and then drain away, leaving it deathly pale as she picked up her skirts and ran toward the hall.

"No. Kate, pull yourself together. The children are fine, as far as I know. That isn't why Blaise is here."

But she doubted if her daughter even heard her. Ah, well, perhaps it wasn't such a bad thing at that.

Blaise was staring into the fire when the door burst open and she was there, like Aurora, with her lovely hair a vibrant fiery cloud about her face, exactly as she had appeared at their first stormy meeting.

"What has happened? One of the children is hurt . . . ill . . . Or, is it your mother? Oh, please, you must tell me!"

He stood up slowly, unable to take his eyes off her.

"My dear," said her father, sounding amused as he rose and walked toward the door, "I believe you have reduced our guest to silence, so allow me to set your mind at rest—no one is ill or in trouble. As to why Blaise is here, I shall leave him to explain, as I am convinced he will do to your full satisfaction."

Neither of them heard the door close behind him, for she was already in Blaise's arms and being kissed until she was breathless.

"I have been all kinds of a fool," Blaise murmured, when both were finally obliged to draw breath. "Oh, Kate—I do want you quite desperately! Can you ever forgive me—be my wife?"

Kate leaned back in his arms so that she could look into his eyes. "I'm not sure about the forgiving. How long a time am I allowed in which to answer?"

"Twenty years? Thirty years? A lifetime." He laughed indulgently, his eyes deeply quizzical and loving at the same time. "How long do you want?"

Kate clasped her hands behind his head to draw it down.

"A lifetime will do very nicely," she murmured softly.